Wait!

Wait!

"It was a dark and stormy night ..."

26 fun and scary stories!!

Presented by

Tayla Tollefson

Cover art created by Tami Hennessy
www.hbsanitarium.com

Library of Congress Control Number: 2019919612
ISBN: Hardcover   978-1-7960-7434-5
             Softcover   978-1-7960-7433-8
             eBook   978-1-7960-7432-1

Print information available on the last page.

Rev. date: 12/02/2019

To order additional copies of this book, contact:
Xlibris
1-888-795-4274
www.Xlibris.com
Orders@Xlibris.com
805935

Table of Contents

To: My Family

Thank You ... Grandpa

For: All readers who love scary stories that are fun.

Foreword

"Okay, kids, just one more story before bedtime," Grandpa would say.

When my little brother and I were young, we would beg our grandpa to tell us a story before we went to sleep. We would snuggle down under the covers and he would make up such wonderful stories. We called them our *dark and stormy night stories.*

Even though we are older now, we still remember what an adventure our grandpa made our bedtimes by telling us his stories. We have never forgotten them and we have treasured them all our lives. We still love the stories, so I asked him to help me write them down so that others might enjoy his awesome bedtime stories.

Here, I am presenting twenty-six of his stories for kids from six to sixty. I'm sure you will love them as much as my brother and I did. I hope my grandpa's stories will become treasures for you too.

... Tayla Tollefson

It was a dark and stormy night ...

Alex and Andrew

Alex and Andrew were visiting their grandparents in Pennsylvania. The favorite part of the trip for the brothers, besides seeing their mother's parents, was the train ride. They had taken the train to visit every summer since they could remember. When they were younger, their mother made the trip with them, but the past three years, they made the trip without her.

Now that Alex was eleven years old and Andrew was ten, they felt 'grown-up' taking the train alone. They liked the feeling of being 'on their own' and riding the train across the country from Montana.

Their parents met years ago while attending the University of Montana in Missoula. They got married and stayed in Montana after college to settle down and have their family. The family ended up being only four of them. Alex and Andrew were the only children in the family. Their mother liked to say that she was glad she didn't have the ten children she dreamed of when she was younger.

Their granddad picked them up at the train station and drove them out to the house. The spooky part of the trip, which always fascinated them, was the drive down the narrow road through the dense forest that led to the house at the end of the road.

They held their breath as they turned the last bend in the road and came within sight of the house. Their grandparents called it 'the homestead' but the boys called it 'the castle' because the big, three-story house, complete with turrets, looked just like some of the castles they had seen in old books.

They liked to explore in the forest surrounding the house, but they had always been cautious about looking around inside the house. There were rooms and areas of the big place that they had never seen. They were just a little too afraid to wander around the old mansion. Inside, it always seemed a little too dark and a little too eerie. It didn't feel like a welcoming place. The boys were sure there were ghosts, although they had never seen them. But, they were almost certain that they had heard them at one time or another. There were also old structures that granddad called 'the outbuildings' scattered around the property that they had never been into.

Since the place was so mysterious, they always went everywhere together while they were visiting. Alex said it was 'safety-in-numbers' and Andrew didn't care about the numbers, he was just glad to be with Alex at all times. But, the castle was also very interesting. Their mother said it was 'charming' but the boys didn't see it quite that way.

They kind of liked the gargoyles that were outside, up on the turrets, but they weren't about to go up there to see them up close. Inside there were big portraits and tapestries on the walls and there was a suit of armor standing in the entry hall. The library had many shelves full of dusty old books and the furniture looked like it was probably made thousands of years ago. It wasn't 'charming' to the boys.

The stairway leading upstairs was steep and it had a really great bannister that they liked a whole lot. Their grandparents always said that it was okay to slide down it. They had slid down that bannister probably a gazillion times. It had always made them laugh to be able to do that. It was really fun.

Upstairs, their bedroom was right at the top of the stairs. It was a big room with two gigantic beds and it had a big fireplace. They liked that.

The hallway was dark and creepy. Even though the boys had visited for years, they had never been down the hallway, not in either direction. Their mother always stayed in the room next to them so they never had to go down the hall to her room. They were afraid of what they would find if they ventured too far. They made up stories about what they might find down at the end of the ghostly hallway.

When they arrived at the house, their grandma heard the car coming up the road and she came out to greet them. They loved seeing her. She was very cheerful and she was always smiling. They hugged her and she kissed them all over their faces. They pretended not to like it, but secretly, they loved grandma's hugs and kisses.

That night, while they were having dinner, it started to rain. Granddad called it a 'squall' but the brothers called it a storm. Granddad said he was glad he had put the horses and cows in the barn and shooed the chickens and ducks into their little houses. They had a couple of pigs, but they liked the rain, so they stayed out so they could make some mud to wallow around in. There were only a few animals on the property.

The rain seemed like it went from a steady rain to some kind of downpour. Then the lightning and the thunder came. To the boys, that was no 'squall' out there – it was a great big storm.

The boys spent a couple of hours playing Monopoly with their grandparents. That was their favorite game and they had brought it with them in Alex's suitcase. They weren't sure their grandparents could appreciate the awesomeness of the game, but they cheerfully played with the brothers because they were so glad to have them visit every summer.

At the end of the game their grandparents seemed to be getting tired, so the boys said that *they* were tired, which was a good excuse for their grandparents to go to bed. Their grandma gave them some candles. She said that, if the storm got worse, they might lose power in the house and they would be glad they had the candles. She said she kept candle holders in their room, but that they'd need fresh candles for them. She said they would find matches on the fireplace.

The brothers went up to their room. They stopped to slide down the bannister a couple of times because they couldn't let the opportunity go by without 'polishing the board' as their grandma put it.

Alex liked to work puzzles so he had brought a nice, thick puzzle book with him from home. Andrew liked to draw and he had brought his 'supplies' with him, so they had stuff to do in their room to keep them busy during the times they were upstairs.

The storm raged on outside, with the lightning and the thunder keeping up a steady pace. Andrew said he hoped it would pass over and move on because he wasn't sure he could sleep with all the racket the storm was making. Alex said that, after the hectic day they had, he didn't think either one of them would have trouble sleeping.

The suddenness of the lightning and thunder made them jump sometimes. Even though they knew it was coming, they were still startled when a big crack of lightning lit up the window in the room.

"Wait! Hey, Andy, did you hear something?" Alex asked, looking up from his puzzle book.

"No, I don't think so," Andrew replied.

"Listen for a minute," Alex said in a whisper.

Andrew stopped drawing in his sketch pad and listened closely for whatever Alex had heard.

"Do you hear it yet?" Alex asked. "I'm sure I can hear something."

Andrew listened. "Wait!" he said. He thought he could hear music. It sounded faint but he was sure that it was some kind of music.

"Hear it?" Alex asked again, speaking in a hushed tone. They were both whispering.

"Yeah," Andrew answered, "it sounds like music."

"Exactly," Alex said. "It's ghost music!"

"What's ghost music?" Andrew asked.

"That's the sounds that ghosts make," Alex said. "It's got to be ... have you ever heard anything like it before?"

Andrew listened for a minute or two.

"Am I right, or what?" Alex insisted.

"I guess," Andrew agreed. "I've never heard it before; real ghost music – wow!"

"It sounds like it might be coming from the attic," Alex said. "We should check it out."

"No way!" wide-eyed Andrew said. "There ain't no way I'm going up into the attic. We've never been up there and this ain't no time to go looking around, especially if ghosts are up there making some kind of spooky music!"

"No," Alex argued, "we've got to go see what it is. It'll be something to tell the guys back home."

"No way, no how," Andrew said.

"Well, if you won't go with me, then I'll have to go by myself," Alex said. "And I'll be forced to tell all your friends that you chickened out," he added to persuade his brother. "You can stay here *all* alone."

"Oh, that's not fair," Andrew said. He wasn't convinced that Alex's idea was even remotely good. "What are you going to do if you find some ghosts?"

"Duh – run!" Alex said jokingly. "C'mon, maybe we won't have to go all the way. Let's just find out where it's coming from."

"Okay, I'll go," Andrew said. He decided that he would rather be in danger with his brother than be left there in the room all by himself.

"Get some candles," Alex instructed. "We're going to need some light and we don't want to turn on the hall light."

"Okay," Andrew said, "but, if the candles blow out I'm running right back here and locking the door. If you get stuck out in the hall then it'll be too bad for you. I'm not opening that door."

"You'd recognize my voice," Alex explained. "You'll know it's me and you can open the door. I'll jump in and slam the door behind me."

"No, it could be the ghost mimicking your voice," Andrew argued. "I'm not taking any chances. Just so you know."

"Okay, fine," Alex said. "I'll just have to beat you back here, before you can slam the door in my face."

"Sorry," Andrew said, "but you know that when I'm scared I only think about saving myself."

"Yeah, I know," Alex answered. "C'mon, let's go."

The brothers went to the door and crept quietly out into the hallway. They left the door open in case they had to make a hasty retreat from their venture.

"Hey," Alex whispered, "It's not the attic. It's coming from down there. We don't need the candles."

He pointed toward the end of the hallway. Andrew followed his pointing finger and he could see an eerie glow from a room at the end of the hall.

"What's down there?" he whispered.

"I don't know," Alex whispered back. "We've never been down there. Let's go look."

Andrew walked close to Alex as the brothers slowly made their way down the hallway. They passed several doors along the way and they paused at each one and listened. They wondered what was in the rooms, but they weren't about to go into them.

As they got closer to the room at the end of the hall, they could see that the door was open and a lamp was on inside the room somewhere. They could tell that they wouldn't be able to see into the room unless they stepped through the doorway. As they approached the open doorway, Alex went to step forward, but Andrew grabbed his arm and pulled him back.

"Wait!" he hissed. "You can't just go right into the room like that! Are you crazy?"

"Well, we've got to see," Alex whispered quietly. "How else are we going to see if we don't go in there?"

"You can't just go in there!" Andrew pleaded. "You don't know what's in there. What if you bust in on a bunch of ghosts – then what?"

"Okay," Alex whispered, "All right, then I'll just peek around the corner."

"Okay," Andrew said, letting go of his brother's arm and taking a step back. "I'm going to be ready to run."

"Yeah, you do that," Alex replied.

"No, seriously," Andrew said, "I'm not kidding. I must be crazy for letting you talk me into this. I'm scared. Don't you understand?"

"Yeah," Alex whispered, "but we're here now so we might as well find out what's going on."

The two brothers stood still for a few minutes listening to the eerie music coming from inside the room. It sounded like music from a long, long time ago – that's how they knew it was ghost music. They were convinced that it really was ghost music because it didn't sound like anything they had ever heard in their lifetimes. They decided it must be from a hundred years ago – maybe two hundred years ago.

"Ready?" Alex asked, after a few minutes.

"Sure," Andrew whispered, but he wasn't the least bit confident. He was terrified of what Alex was going to find when he peeked around the corner. He was terrified of what could happen to his brother – he might straighten up without his head! The thought horrified him and he was even more afraid than he thought it was possible to be.

Andrew held his breath as Alex leaned slowly toward the door jamb and peeked around the edge of the doorway. He almost jumped when Alex let out a soft sound, straightened up, and leaned against the wall next to the doorway. His eyes were closed, but Andrew could see he at least still had his head.

"What?" he whispered, urgently. "What is it?"

Alex didn't answer right away. Andrew worried that he could be in a trance or something. He shook his brother forcefully.

"Alex," he hissed. "What is it? What's in there?"

Then Alex opened his eyes and looked at his brother.

"What is it?" Andrew insisted. "What happened?"

"Nothing," Alex answered. Then he smiled. "It's nothing. See for yourself."

"No way," Andrew breathed loudly.

"No, really," Andrew said. "Have a look. You won't know unless you see for yourself," he urged.

Andrew was scared, but he leaned toward the doorway and peeked around the corner into the room. He let out his breath as he stepped back and leaned against the wall next to Alex.

He had seen his granddad asleep in a big chair. Next to the chair, on a table, was an old phonograph. It had a big turntable that was going around and around. On the phonograph was one of grandad's old records. He had called them his 'old 78 Rpms' a few times. The brothers had seen them before but they had never heard them played.

Granddad told them they wouldn't like the music on them because it was from 'back in the day' and they wouldn't be able to appreciate the music after hearing the junk played on the radio nowadays. He always said that what was played nowadays wasn't really music but that people had gotten used to it. Progress, he said, was humbug.

To the brothers, in the middle of the night, in a big storm, it sounded like ghost music to them. But, now they knew what was at the end of the hall.

The End

It was a dark and stormy night ...

Bartholomew

Bartholomew ... he wasn't exactly crazy about the name he had been given. It was hard for him to say when he was little, and even harder for him to write when he started school and was learning to write.

His dad liked telling him the story about how he got his name. He said that he was named after a character in a book that he read *way, way* back when *he* was a child. Then his dad would laugh and wink, like he wanted Bartholomew to believe that way, way back meant that he was like hundreds of years old.

Bartholomew had fallen for the joke at first but, somewhere along the way, he realized that it wasn't possible for anyone to be *that* old. So, after he understood that fact, he wasn't fooled anymore. It became just one of the old stories that his dad would tell ... like the one about how his family travelled across the country in a covered wagon long, long ago and discovered California.

He liked his dad's stories – that is, the ones that didn't include him. Sometimes his dad would stick him into the story – like the one about when the family went to the moon and found out that it was made of cheese and Bartholomew had eaten so much that he got sick ...

because the moon was made of green cheese ... a kind that you can't eat.

When Bartholomew was about six years old, he realized that the stories were made up because they seemed too farfetched to really be true. His dad told him that he always put Bartholomew into the stories to make sure he was listening and to make the stories seem more interesting.

But, his dad wanted him to know the story of how he got his name and to know that it was actually true. The book was about a kid who had 500 hats. It was his dad's favorite story as a kid and he decided that when he grew up and had a son, he would name him Bartholomew.

He wanted to be called Bart. To him, it sounded like it belonged to a stronger, tougher person. His mother was the only one who still called him Bartholomew – when he did something wrong or when she wanted to get his 'undivided' attention.

Now, today, Bart was *so* bored. His best friend, Devlin, was away on vacation with his family. School was out for the summer and he didn't have anything to do. The weather had turned really bad and a storm had rolled into the neighborhood. The thunder was really loud and scary. The lightning was bad enough that his parents wouldn't allow him to go outside. The rain came down in buckets – his grandmother said it was raining cats and dogs. He had heard her say that before and he had never seen any animals falling with the rain. Now he knew exactly where his dad got his storytelling talent.

He knew there wouldn't be any outside activities that day. He had tried to keep himself busy all day. He read for a while, he played darts in the garage for a while, and he worked on a dusty, old jigsaw puzzle he found on his bookshelf. It had been on that shelf for a long time. He had promised himself that he would put it together sooner or later, but he had never found the time. Then, he cleaned his room and did some other chores that his mother gave him to do. He watched television for a time but it didn't keep his attention. After hours and hours and more hours, he ran out of things to do.

He decided that if the long, long day didn't end soon, he might have to start pulling out his hair for something to do. It seemed like just about the longest day of his life.

Normally, he would be with Devlin. When they weren't able to go outside with their skateboards or basketball or Frisbee, they would spend time at each other's house and find things to do indoors. It seemed like they could always think of something to do.

Devlin lived directly across the street. They had been very best friends ever since kindergarten when Devlin's family moved into the neighborhood. There weren't any other young boys in the neighborhood at the time and Bart was so glad to meet him. There were some girls who lived on his street, but it wasn't the same thing as having a guy to hang around with.

The two boys were the same age and they became instant friends. Since then, they had spent all of their time together. Every night, before they went to bed, they would signal each other across the street from their windows with flashlights. They made up their own secret signal code when they were eight years old and they had only missed a few nights in the past three years.

They missed one time when Devlin had his tonsils taken out and once when Bart had to have his appendix taken out. Besides those two times, the only times they ever missed was when their families went away on vacation.

The rain stopped just after dinner and the storm moved on to somewhere else. Bart looked out of his bedroom window and saw that fog was drifting into the neighborhood. It looked like it was pretty heavy. It was settling around the houses and wrapping around the trees like it was sticky. It looked spooky out there. He could barely see across the street.

Bart looked over at Devlin's house. It was dark over there. The house was covered in fog. It looked like a blanket was wrapped around it. He couldn't see the downstairs windows at all. He thought the dark, empty house looked lonely and cold. He was lonely too, just looking at it. He missed his best friend. He decided he would just pretend that Devlin was over there in his room and he would signal to him before he went to bed – just like a regular night. He thought it would make him feel better if he acted like Devlin was there … even if he didn't signal back. He could just make believe that he *did* signal back.

Bart turned out his bedroom light so the room would be dark and his signal would be seen better, just like he did every night. He got his flashlight and went to the window. He turned it on and pointed it toward Devlin's window. He pressed the button to blink the light that would spell out their code. It *did* make him feel better. It made him feel so much better that he signaled again. Then he signaled once more.

Suddenly, there was a light in Devlin's window and it was blinking! At first, Bart was excited to think that maybe Devlin had come home and he was signaling back. Bart signaled again and the light in Devlin's window answered.

"Wait! It's the wrong signal," he said out loud. It wasn't their code! Something wasn't right! When the light blinked again, Bart was suddenly scared. He dropped down on the floor below the window. He was afraid of someone seeing him. It wasn't Devlin! He slowly raised his head so he could peek over the edge of the window. Sure enough, the light blinked again.

Bart was terrified! Someone was in Devlin's room and they were using his flashlight to signal! He knew that Devlin's family was gone out of town. Who could be over there?

Bart peeked over the edge of the window again. Devlin's window was dark – the light wasn't blinking anymore. He watched for a few minutes. There was no light. Maybe he imagined it, he thought to himself. Maybe what he saw was his own light reflecting on Devlin's window. Yeah, that had to be it, he decided. That was the simple explanation. That was easy to understand. He had just made a mistake, that's all.

He decided that he would shine his light on Devlin's window and move it around. That way, he could see that it was just his light shining on the glass and it would prove he had made a mistake.

Bart got up on his knees and shined his light across the street. When his light hit the window of Devlin's room, he moved it around and around in a circle. He could see the pattern he was making.

Wait! All of a sudden, the blinking light flashed again! Bart dropped flat on the floor and crawled to the side of his window. Oh, no, he thought, he hadn't made a mistake! Someone was over there! He was more scared than ever. He inched up close to the window and peeked around the curtain. The light was still blinking! Now he was certain. A monster or something was in Devlin's room!

What could it be? How could a monster get into Devlin's house? Wait a minute – he had seen a movie where there was a vampire next door and a boy saw him from his window. The vampire tried to get the boy to come over so he could attack him.

That's it! That had to be it! A vampire got into Devlin's house and now it knew he had seen it. It would probably wait until he was asleep and come after him. He was terrified. His knees felt wobbly. He felt very tired all of a sudden. Was the vampire putting a spell on him? That was it! The vampire was making him feel sleepy so he couldn't get away when it came after him. Vampires had that power, right? Bart thought that he learned that from the movie. Vampires could put you under a spell so you would do what they want!

He had to go tell his dad! He was afraid he wouldn't be able to move. He felt heavy and sleepy. But, if he didn't go for help, the vampire would get him, he decided. He *had* to move, he told himself. He forced his feet to move and he inched his way around the edge of the room in the dark. He was careful not to pass in front of the window. He slowly crept toward the door.

When he reached the doorway, he ran down the hall to his parents' room. The room was empty! His parents were still awake. They were downstairs. He backed out of their room and ran down the stairs to the living room.

"Dad," he shouted when he entered the room, "there's a vampire in Devlin's house!"

"Whoa, there, Sport," his dad said, throwing up his hands. "What's brought this on?"

"Dad, I signaled with my flashlight and someone answered back with Devlin's flashlight," Bart said. He was breathing heavily.

"Whoa," his dad said, "catch your breath and tell me what's going on. You know Devlin's family is out of town. There's no one over there. They won't be back until next week."

Bart stopped and took a couple of deep breaths. "Yeah, Dad," he answered, "I know, but I signaled over there to Devlin's window, just like I always do because I was pretending that Devlin was there and someone signaled back using his flashlight. I think it might be a vampire and he knows that I saw him. He's trying to put a spell on me! He's going to come after me because I saw him!"

His parents looked at each other and then his dad looked back toward Bart. He smiled and said, "I don't think vampires come out until later in the night." He winked at Bart's mother.

"No, Dad," Bart pleaded, "I'm serious. There's a vampire or something over there in Devlin's house. It signaled back with his flashlight. Really, I'm not kidding!"

His dad asked, "What do you want me to do about it, son?"

"I don't know," Bart answered, "call the police or something!"

"I'll go over and check it out," his dad replied. "I have the key to their house. I'll go find out what's going on."

"No, Dad, you can't go over there! What if the vampire is waiting for you? He'll get you. Don't go!" Bart begged.

"You wait here and watch your mother and I'll be back in a few minutes," his dad said, getting up from his chair. He went into the hallway, picked up the key for Devlin's house from the hall table, and went out the front door. Bart sat down next to his mother and she put her arm around him.

"Don't worry," she said. "It'll be okay. Your dad's a tough old guy. You don't have to worry about him. He'll be just fine."

Bart was still afraid, not only for himself, but especially for his dad. He wondered if his dad could fight off a vampire without being put under a spell.

It seemed like his dad was gone for a long time. Bart worried when he didn't come back right away. After about ten minutes they heard the front door open and close. Bart breathed a sigh of relief when he saw his dad in the doorway. He came in and sat down in his chair.

"What happened?" Bart almost yelled. "Was it a vampire? Did you kill it?"

"No," his dad answered. "It's nothing like that. It's just Devlin's cousin. He's here from college and he's housesitting for Devlin's family while they're on vacation. He said that he's sleeping in Devlin's room. He said someone over here was shining a light in the window so he just answered back. So, there's no vampire or monster. Everything's fine."

Bart was relieved. He couldn't wait to tell Devlin.

The End

It was a dark and stormy night ...

Cameron and Paul

"Wait!" Paul said suddenly, looking up from the card game they were playing in the tent. "Did you hear something?"

"No," Cameron answered, "I wasn't listening for anything. I was thinking about the game. You heard something? What was it?"

"I don't know, it sounded like something walking around out there," Paul whispered. "Something was rustling and moving around."

"I didn't hear it," Cameron whispered back. "Want me to take a look and see?"

"NO!" Paul said hurriedly. "It could be a monster."

"A monster," Cameron said, "like what?"

"Maybe it's the Wombat," Paul said.

"Oh," Cameron said, shaking his head up and down like he agreed that it was a possibility.

"Remember last summer at camp?" Paul asked. "They told us not to go outside the tent after dark because the Wombat would get you."

"Yeah, I remember," Cameron answered. "Do you think it could really be out there?"

"Maybe," Paul said. "Just listen for a minute."

The two boys sat quietly, holding their breath, and listening closely.

"Hey," Cameron said in a low tone, "I think you might be right. I can hear something moving around out there now."

They were leaning toward each other and they were speaking in low, soft tones. They were starting to get nervous.

"It's prowling around the tent. Probably looking for a way to get in," Paul offered.

"Good thing we pulled the zipper on the door all the way closed," Cameron said as he looked toward the flap that served as a door to their tent.

The boys looked at each other, almost holding their breath. They listened keenly for any sounds outside the tent.

It was Saturday night and Cameron and Paul were 'camping out' in Cameron's backyard in a tent his uncle gave him for his birthday. Their parents didn't think that two ten-year-old boys should be out in the yard alone overnight.

The boys promised them there wasn't anything to worry about. They practically begged. Then they tried another tactic. They tried to reason with their parents. They were trying to make it sound like it was no big deal, but it actually was, because they had never camped out in the yard before.

"But, we'll be out in our own backyard," Cameron said to them. "We'll be right out there where you can see us anytime you look out."

"I'm not sure about this," Paul's mother said.

"But, the whole backyard is fenced in," Paul said.

"Well, then," Cameron's mother started to say something, but that was as far as she got.

"We'll be okay," Paul interrupted.

"Please, Mom, please," Cameron pleaded. "We'll be right there." He pointed out the window to the big tree in the backyard.

Cameron's mother had her arms folded in front of her. He knew it meant that she was undecided. She could be stubborn when she wasn't sure about something.

"Oh, Jeannie," Cameron's father said. "I'm sure they'll be fine out there. There's nothing out there that can harm them."

"Well," Cameron's mother said, throwing up her arms, "if you feel comfortable with it, then I guess it's all right with me too."

"And me," Paul's mother added.

"Yay!" Paul said, hugging his mother. His father wasn't there. He was out of town on a business trip.

"Yeah," Cameron said, "and we promise to come into the house if anything happens."

Their parents were still a little concerned because a storm was coming. The boys were quick to point out that the tent was waterproof. They were sure they would stay dry.

Cameron's father explained that the concern wasn't the rain, but the lightning. They were worried about the lightning that would come with the storm.

The boys went out and set up the tent in the afternoon, but their parents wouldn't let them go out there until the lightning had passed over.

"What do you think it is?" Paul asked. "I think it has to be the Wombat. What else can it be?"

"It's probably the storm," Cameron answered. "It's kind of windy. I'm hoping that that's what it is. I keep wondering what else it can be, but I can't think of anything else that's going to be out in the yard."

"But, the wind doesn't walk around," Paul said. He thought that made very good sense. "It's the Wombat I tell you. It's a crazy monster and it's creeping around because it saw us come out here."

"Don't get scared yet," Cameron whispered. "We don't know for sure what it is."

"Should we go in?" Paul's eyes were open wide in fright. He was getting more frightened by what he was thinking – and also by what his imagination was creating in his mind.

"No!" Cameron said quietly, but strongly. "If we chicken out now and go into the house, we'll prove that our parents were right. They won't ever let us camp out again. Besides, we've only been out here for an hour. Let's wait and see."

Paul said, "So, you think we'll be okay?"

"So far, so good," Cameron answered. "If it was some crazy monster it probably would have ripped in here by now. Maybe it'll go away."

The boys sat listening to the storm outside. They were glad the thunder and lightning from earlier had passed on. If they were still there, with all the noise they made during a storm, the boys wouldn't have been able to hear the monster outside the tent.

The rain was still there. It had been heavy at first and then it got lighter as the storm moved away. Now it was what they called sprinkling. It was still a little windy. The boys could hear the wind blowing. After a few minutes they heard the rustling again.

"See," Paul said. "I'm telling you that something is out there – and it doesn't sound like it's going to go away!"

"You're right," Cameron said softly. "I can hear it too. Good thing I brought my BB gun along."

"What should we do?" Paul was looking even more scared now. He could feel his heart beating faster.

"Just wait, for now," Cameron said.

"What, wait in here until the Wombat comes in and gets us?" Paul said. He was anxious.

"It can't get in here," Cameron responded, trying to calm his friend down.

"Duh," Paul said. "The tent is only made of nylon! It's not like it's made of steel or anything! That Wombat has sharp claws. It can rip right through."

Cameron was getting more scared. To him, wide-eyed Paul was looking terrified. He felt like they had to do something before Paul started screaming and running for the house.

"Why don't I unzip the flap a little and shoot out with the BB gun," Cameron offered. "That might scare it away."

"Good," Paul said. "That might be a good idea. I'll look. You do the shooting."

Cameron got the BB gun. He checked it to make sure it was ready. Paul unzipped the flap a couple of inches and peeked out.

Cameron asked, "See anything?"

"No, it might be around the side or something," Paul whispered.

"Let me look," Cameron said, as he crawled over to the tent flap. He peered out through the opening into the dark. "I don't see anything either," he said really quietly.

He stuck the end of the gun barrel out through the hole and fired. It didn't make a very loud sound.

"What do you think?" he asked Paul.

"It wasn't very loud," Paul answered. "Maybe you should do it again."

Cameron cocked the gun and poked it through the opening. He fired it again and pulled it back in. They didn't hear anything.

"Did it sound like it ran away?" Cameron asked.

"No, I didn't hear anything running away," Paul said, leaning forward to listen.

They heard the rustling again. Cameron peeked out the opening.

"I think I see it," he said. "I can see its shadow. I think it's in the tree."

Paul gasped. "It means that it's right over the tent, right on top of us!"

Cameron zipped up the opening and the boys scrambled into their sleeping bags. They lay perfectly still, facing each other.

"What should we do now?" Paul whispered.

"Just lie still and if it can't hear us, maybe it will go away," Cameron whispered back.

"I'm kind of scared," Paul said softly.

"Me too," Cameron agreed.

"Maybe we should go in," Paul suggested.

"No, we can't," Cameron argued. "We promised that we would stick it out because they won't let us stay out again if they find out we were scared."

"Okay, then," Paul whispered.

The boys lay quietly, listening to the rustling outside, and to the wind that wasn't as strong as it was earlier.

They moved their sleeping bags close together. They looked at each other but they didn't talk. They wanted to be just as quiet as possible. After a while of listening so intently, the exhausted boys fell asleep.

"Cam?" a voice said. "Cam, are you awake?"

The boys woke up to the sound of Cameron's dad calling from outside the tent.

They sat up and looked around. It was morning. They were very pleased to see that they had survived the night. The Wombat didn't tear its way into the tent after all. They were feeling lucky.

"Cam," his father called again.

Cameron unzipped the tent flap and looked out at his father.

"Hi, Dad," he said. "What are you doing out here?"

"I just wanted to see if you brought your BB gun out here with you," his father said.

"Yeah, we brought it for protection, just in case," Cameron answered.

"Well ... did you have a *just-in-case moment* and decide to shoot the gun?" he asked plainly.

"Yeah," Cameron said. "We heard a Wombat and we fired a couple of times to scare it away."

"A Wombat?" his father sounded doubtful.

"Yeah, we heard it prowling around outside so we were trying to scare it off," Cameron explained.

"I thought so," His father said. "I thought I heard a couple of BBs hitting the window of the house."

"The window broke?" Cameron asked.

"No, the window didn't break," his father answered, and he smiled. "I thought I recognized the sound from when I used to have my own BB gun."

"Whew," Cameron breathed. "I'm glad of that. I didn't think we were shooting that way."

"Was the Wombat scared away?" his dad asked.

"No, I don't think so," Cameron said. "The gun isn't very loud, so I guess it wasn't surprised enough to run away. We just stayed in here where it was safe."

"Wombat, you say," his father added.

"Yeah, Mr. Matthews," Paul said. "They told us about the Wombat at camp. It prowls around at night in the dark, looking for a way to get into your tent and eat you!"

"Boys," he said, "wombats live in Australia. That's thousands and thousands of miles from here. I doubt if your wombat could travel the distance."

"But it can, Dad," Cameron put in. "It was at camp last summer and last night we heard it out here in the yard. We heard it rusting around right outside the tent. It was in the tree right over us."

"Son, the wombat only lives in Australia, nowhere else," his father explained. "It's a little bear that lives in the ground. It's a vegetarian. It wouldn't be in the tree and it wouldn't eat you."

"But, we heard it," Paul said. "It's probably gone now because the sun is out."

"Come on out here you two," Cameron's father said, waving his hand. "Let me show you something."

The boys crawled out of the tent and stood up.

"What is it?" Paul asked.

"Yeah, is it footprints?" Cameron asked.

"No, there's no footprints," his dad answered. He pointed up into the tree. "Look up there."

The boys looked and saw a plastic grocery bag clinging to the tree branches.

"There's your rustling Wombat," he said smiling. "The prowling monster was just a plastic bag. The wind most likely blew it across the yard and it got stuck on the tree limb. The bag was blowing in the wind and scraping across the branches as it waved."

"Oh, we were scared for nothing," Paul said, breathing a big sigh of relief. "We were too afraid to come out and look."

"That's fine," Cameron's father said, "but, there's always a good explanation for things that happen. Next time, just try to figure out what it could be instead of jumping to conclusions like that. Your imagination can scare you for nothing.

"Uh, next time?" Cameron turned toward his father. "We can stay out again?"

"Sure," he said, "we just won't mention this to anyone. Your mother won't have to worry. We'll just let her think that you two were fine out here ... and you really were. You braved it out, and that should be rewarded with a second chance."

"Thanks, Dad," Cameron said.

"Yeah, Mr. Matthews," Paul chimed in, "thanks a lot." And he was already looking forward to their next camping trip in Cameron's backyard.

The End

It was a dark and stormy night ...

Doris

It was a wet and rainy evening. Heavy clouds were hanging low in the sky, making everything very dark and foggy. The wind was cold and biting. Doris looked out through the store window. It was kind of spooky outside, she thought to herself. The heavy rain that fell earlier had flooded some of the streets and encouraged shoppers to stay home. The rain had eased up some but there were pools of water along the sidewalks and in the streets.

Doris buttoned up her coat and wrapped her scarf around her neck. She pulled her hood up over her head and went out onto the sidewalk in front of the store. She realized that she was kind of nervous and a little bit frightened to walk alone down the foggy, near deserted streets.

She had an errand to run. There wasn't anyone else to do it. It didn't seem like a problem. It was just an errand. It shouldn't take her long, she thought.

In her purse was the bank bag from the department store where she worked. The bag was filled with money. Tonight was the first time she had been asked to make the bank deposit because the person who usually took care of that was out sick from work. Since she wasn't really in a hurry to get home, she had agreed to make the deposit for her boss. She was supposed to place the bank bag in the night deposit box at the front of the bank.

The bank was four blocks from the store. She thought that perhaps she should call a taxi to take her there, but she decided it would be just as easy to simply walk down to the bank and make the deposit. Then, she could walk back toward the store and catch a later bus than she usually took to go home. For goodness sake, she said to herself, it was only four blocks. That shouldn't take very long at all, she reasoned.

Doris looked up and down the street. It was deserted all right. The street was very quiet for the time of evening. It couldn't be more than six o'clock, but the storm made it so much darker than usual. There was hardly any traffic either. Plus, the fog was making it look creepy.

She turned and started walking toward the bank. She splashed in the puddles on the sidewalk as she clutched her overcoat about her shoulders. She hunched her shoulders against the wind and the light drizzle of rain.

She hurried along, occasionally turning her head as a bright window display caught her eye. She had walked about two blocks when ... Wait! She thought she heard the sound of footsteps on the sidewalk behind her. Leaning her head to one side, she listened closely to identify the sounds, but the wind made it difficult for her to hear clearly. She wasn't exactly sure what the sounds were. After a few minutes the sounds came closer and then she recognized them as footsteps. Yes, they were definitely footsteps!

Doris glanced back over her shoulder to make sure her mind wasn't playing tricks on her. There was a man behind her! She could see him walking along the sidewalk through the fog. He was going in the same direction as she was. She wondered if he was following her. Was he just passing this way? She didn't know why, but she was suddenly frightened. What would anyone be doing out on a night like this?

She tried to reason with herself to help her calm down. Maybe he just got off the bus and was simply walking home, she thought. Maybe he lived in the apartment complex that she knew was up ahead. She passed it on the bus every morning and evening. But, if he lived in the apartments, why didn't he get off the bus closer to the complex? Well, she argued with herself, he had every right to be out. The street didn't belong to just her. Anyone could be out walking. It wasn't that late ... right?

She heard the steps again. Fear washed over her and all of her reasoning left her. She felt cold and very scared. She felt little tingles of fear running up and down her body. No, she assured herself, there shouldn't be anyone out in this weather. Why would anyone be out, exactly on the night when she had to go to the bank?

Her imagination took over and it ran crazy wild. No ... he must be following her, she figured. Yes, that's it ... sure, that's exactly it ... he was following her! She was positive. She was so sure of it! It was so obvious to her. He was trying to catch up to her! That's why he was walking faster and faster. He was stalking her! She walked faster.

Oh my goodness, she decided, he knew she was carrying all this money and he wanted it! But, how could he know that she had the money? He couldn't possibly know, could he? But, at that point she was beyond being rational. She didn't care how he knew. She was convinced that he did know and that she was in trouble.

She was suddenly very terrified and she was having trouble breathing. She couldn't seem to catch her breath. She thought her heart must be up in her throat. She was afraid to look back to see how close he was to her.

Doris started walking even faster and the steps behind her quickened. Oh, he's walking faster too! At that moment she was absolutely certain that he was after her. She was ready-to-scream frightened. Oh, why, oh, why did she ever agree to carry this money to the bank?

As she speeded up, he did too. Was he catching up to her? She was certain that he was. He was getting closer with every step, her mind decided. Her breath was coming in short, quick gasps. Oh, no, she thought, he was overtaking her!

She walked still faster! The man behind her started walking faster too! She was horrified and her legs felt weak. She wanted to scream! She opened her mouth but nothing came out. Her throat was closed and she was too afraid to even breathe.

Then, she panicked. She began to run. She forced her wobbly legs to move faster and faster. Her feet were slipping on the wet sidewalk as she ran. The smooth soles of her shoes weren't helping her a bit. Her shoes were making her slide, but, she didn't dare stop. She ran!

Then, she tripped over something and she stumbled. The steps behind her grew louder and they were catching up to her! They were right behind her! Then she lurched forward and fell ... face down on the sidewalk.

The footsteps behind her stopped! The man was standing right directly over her! She couldn't breathe. Then, strong hands closed around each of her arms and she was pulled up to her feet. Oh, no, she thought, this must be the end of her! She was petrified! Shaking, she turned slowly to face the robber. She suddenly recognized him and she fainted.

When she came to, the man was patting her face, trying to wake her up. She opened her eyes and he smiled at her.

Her attacker was David Carter, her boyfriend. He had come down to the store on the bus to surprise her and ride home with her. When he found out that she had already left, heading for the bank, he had followed her. When he saw that she had begun to panic he hurried to catch up to her but he had laryngitis and wasn't able to call out to her.

The End

Eddie

Eddie lived with his family outside of a small town in Arkansas. His house was in a clearing in a forest between the main road and the river.

They would get wood from the forest for the fireplace in the winter. And, when it was hot in the summer, because of the humidity, he would go with his brothers and sisters to swim in the river.

They had all learned early to watch out for the water moccasins that might be in the weeds and in the low-hanging tree branches along the river bank. There were also rattlesnakes in the weeds along the river and in the forest.

Everyone in the family was aware of the threats, but it was a fact of life and they had all grown up knowing of the dangers. It wasn't a big deal. It was just a part of life.

Eddie's family lived on a farm and they knew there were many dangers working and living on a farm. You had to be careful of accidents.

Eddie liked to play in the woods. There was a little creek running through the trees that had petrified wood stuck in its muddy edges. He loved to explore down there, but he wasn't allowed to go into the trees alone because he was only seven years old. But, he had four older brothers who were always willing to go with him when they weren't working.

The whole family worked all year round. They worked for farmers in the area. His daddy said that there were always things to do on the farms and it didn't matter if it was summer or winter, somebody had to do those jobs.

Eddie's brothers worked in the peach or apple orchards, picking the fruit and driving tractors, and his mama and two sisters worked in the sheds where they brought the fruit to be sorted and packaged. Eddie was too young to help. He would just hang around and play while his mama was working.

When there weren't any peaches or apples to pick, there were all kinds of other vegetables: tomatoes, onions, potatoes, bell peppers, and carrots. They picked everything. If it grew in the ground or on a tree, someone around there was growing it, his daddy would say.

There was also farm equipment that his brothers could operate during the harvest. His daddy was the crew supervisor during the harvest for several local farmers who had big farms with lots of stuff growing. They had soy beans and cotton and hay that had to be harvested.

Eddie's brothers would go out to the fields after school and work until dark picking vegetables. The farmers would come along about dusk with a long flat trailer pulled by a tractor. His brothers would follow along beside the trailer and load the bushels of vegetables they had picked and placed at the ends of the rows.

Eddie would go along with them after school and just tag along up and down the rows while they worked.

Sometimes he would try to help, but he wasn't fast enough to keep up. He felt like he was more in the way than helpful, but his brothers never complained about it. They said that he would learn, sooner or later, and at some point he would be able to keep up with them – or even be faster than they were. They urged him to keep trying. They would say that there's money to be made and they wanted to get it while the getting was good.

Each one of his siblings had savings accounts at the bank in town. Their parents insisted that they save money for college so they could get a college degree and they could become something other than farmers. Farming was such hard work.

So, when anyone in the area needed help with anything, they would be right there taking on the job. Whether it was baling hay, shoveling out the barn after the cows lived in there all winter, or digging an irrigation ditch, they were there to do the work and he had never heard a one of them complain.

His daddy said they were fourth generation farmers and it was a hard life. He said that he would like to see his children grow up and be something else. He said it would be nice to have a doctor, or a lawyer, or a business owner in the family. One of his sisters wanted to open a grocery store with her boyfriend after they were married. Eddie's mama told her that she had to finish college so she would know how to run a business and make it work.

All of the kids were determined and they were hard workers. Eddie wasn't sure what he wanted to be when he grew up but his father told him he had plenty of time to decide.

One of his brothers planned to go into the military. He said they give you money to go to college and, together with what he had saved working on the farms, he thought he could pay his way through college. He wanted to be a navy pilot. Then, after the military, he believed he could be a pilot for one of the airline companies. Eddie thought that his brother had his whole life worked out. It seemed like every brother and every sister had decided on a different job. No two planned to be the same thing when they grew up. He thought that was cool.

Eddie shared a room with his brother, Bobby. He dreamed of having his own room. His dream came true when his oldest brother, Virgil, left for college and Eddie was able to move into his room.

Virgil planned to be home on some of the holidays and over the summer. He thought that he could work over the summer and make money for school. His parents decided that, since Bobby's room was larger, when Virgil came home he would stay in the bigger room with Bobby.

Eddie was very pleased with his room. It wasn't as big as the room he shared with Bobby but he had it all to himself and that made him happy.

In his new room, Eddie was able to have his bed right under the window. He loved to look out at the sky at night and see the moon and the stars. In the room with Bobby, his brother, being older, got to choose and so he slept closest to the window.

Now, Eddie could lie in his bed with the shade pulled up and see the moon as it moved across the sky and watch the stars as they moved and changed position in the sky. It was great.

The most disappointing part was when there was a storm. The dark clouds blocked the stars and there was no moon. His daddy said there *was* a moon, but you just couldn't see it because it was behind the clouds.

Looking at the sky at night, Eddie thought he might like to be an astronaut when he grew up and travel up there. Maybe he could go to the moon, maybe to Mars, and to other planets. Or ... maybe he would be a fireman. He hadn't made up his mind. Besides, as his daddy said, he had lots of time to figure it out. His daddy said not to be in a big hurry. He promised him that, at some point, he would discover just what he wanted to do with his life and then he would make it happen.

Also from his new room, he could look out from the second floor window and see the tree tops of the forest surrounding the house. He would sit at the window and watch the lightning bugs flitting back and forth. He wondered what they were looking for and if they talked to each other when they passed another lightning bug that they knew.

He would watch for the fox that would sometimes run across the yard and listen to the frogs and the crickets and the owl that lived out there somewhere. He had never seen the owl but he could hear him at night. He would stay at the window, kneeling on his bed until he got tired and then he would lie down and just drift quietly off to sleep. His mama said it was a natural relaxer for a growing boy after a long day.

Shortly after he moved into the room, he was at the window and he noticed some strange lights out in the trees. He watched them for a while as they moved across the forest, shining up into the tree tops. They didn't last very long. They were brief, but they would go one direction, and a little later they would go back the other way. He didn't know where they disappeared to after going one way and before they went back the other way.

One night, during a storm, he was at the window watching the lightning and watching the rain run off the roof in front of his window. The lightning would light up the trees and make everything out there look really spooky. Whenever there was a storm, fog would appear from somewhere and float around in the trees. It was fascinating because it looked like the fog was trying to float away but the trees were grabbing it and holding it down.

As he was watching the storm, he saw the lights in the treetops again. They passed one way and, a few minutes later, they went back the other way. He watched the lights for a few minutes. He wondered what they could be.

Wait! It suddenly dawned on him what they were! He remembered watching a show on television with his brothers. It was a show about some strange lights in a forest near a military base in England. It was aliens! That's what the television show said they were. They were aliens and some people on the show said the aliens kidnap people and take them away!

He must have forgotten about it because he didn't connect the lights from England to the lights in his forest until that moment.

Aliens! Eddie was suddenly afraid. Aliens were zooming around in the trees behind his house! If they saw him at the window, would they come and get him? Did they already know that he was there? Had they seen him watching them from the window on other nights? Had they decided to kidnap him?

Through the fog and the rain, even though the moon was blocked out by the dark clouds, he could still see the lights. When the lightning from the storm lit up the woods, he strained to see through the fog. He tried to see the aliens out in the trees.

Every time the aliens passed through the trees he became more and more afraid. He wondered what aliens do to people? One of his brothers, Gary, had joked that they were reptiles, like big snakes, and that they eat people. The thought terrified him!

He watched closely for the lights. He tried to tell if they were coming closer to the house. He didn't want to look out the window, but he *had* to know if the aliens were coming after him. He was worried that they were coming closer and he was really scared. What should he do if the aliens flew over to his window? He was too afraid to move. He just kept staring out the window.

He felt the urge to go tell his family. That would be the brave thing to do. He should try to save his family. He really wanted to move but he just couldn't. Did the aliens have him under a spell that made it so he couldn't move? He tried to speak, but his throat was closed. He thought it was probably paralyzed by the spell the aliens were putting on him – he couldn't even swallow.

He was petrified! He could feel the tears forming in his eyes but he wasn't even sure that he could blink his eyes, even if he wanted to.

At that moment, he heard the bedroom door open behind him. He heard his sister, Charlotte's, voice in the doorway.

"Mama wanted me to check on you before I go to bed because of the storm," she said. When he didn't respond, she asked, "What are you staring at out that window?"

She came over and sat down on the bed behind him. She put her hand on his shoulder. "What are you looking at?" she asked. When he still didn't answer she got on the bed on her knees and moved over beside him. She put her arm around him and said, "What is it? Is something out there?"

Eddie nodded his head up and down.

"What is it?" she asked, looking out the window and trying to see whatever he was looking at. "Eddie, you're shaking like a leaf," she said. "What is it?"

Eddie swallowed hard. It was difficult, but he found his voice. "Aliens," he whispered

"Aliens ... where?" She asked, leaning closer to the glass.

"Watch," Eddie said. "Look at the trees. They're aliens! They're trying to kidnap me!"

"Why would they do that? What's giving you that notion?" Charlotte asked.

"I saw it on television," Eddie whispered. "Those lights in the trees are aliens! And when you see them by your house, Gary said that they will kidnap you and eat you. I think they saw me the other night and now they're after me."

"No, there aren't any aliens out there," Charlotte said soothingly

"Sure there are," he insisted, "don't you see their lights out there? It's really aliens! They're after me! They're going to get me. If I disappear in the middle of the night you'll know that it's true and that they kidnapped me!"

"Listen, Eddie," she said, turning his face with her hand so that he was looking at her. "Let me tell you what those lights are. They've always been there. You never saw them before because Bobby's room faces the front of the house."

Eddie didn't say anything.

"Look at the lights with me," Charlotte said.

Eddie turned his face back toward the window.

"Watch," she said. In a few minutes he saw the lights moving through the treetops

"See, those are headlights from cars going by over there," she explained.

"But, they're up in the top of the trees," Eddie said. He was confused.

"No, on the other side of those trees there's a road," Charlotte said. "There's a hill on the road just right there. Cars coming from both directions shine their lights upward when they are coming to the top of the hill. The car lights shine into the tree tops and move along through the trees until the cars get to the top of the hill and start down the other side. Then when a car comes from the other direction, it looks like the same lights going back the other way, but it's actually a different car going in the other direction."

"Are you sure?" Eddie asked.

"I promise," she said. "I used to wonder about them too. My room is next to yours and they scared me too at first. Mama explained what they were. I guess no one thought to tell you about it because it never came up. We all know about it, so there hasn't been any reason. No one pays any attention to them anymore because we know what they are."

"I thought they were aliens and they were going to take me away in their spaceship," Eddie said.

"No, that's not going to happen," Charlotte assured him. "You're perfectly safe and you don't have a thing to worry about."

Eddie felt very relieved. He had let what Gary said scare him half to death. He decided at that moment that his idea about being an astronaut when he grew up was being marked off his list. Being a firefighter was now at the top of that list.

The End

It was a dark and stormy night ...

Frankie

Frankie hurried up the walkway leading to her house. She was holding her umbrella low over her head to protect her backpack. Her backpack was full of books, not only a couple of school books, but six books she had gotten at the school library that day.

When she reached the porch, she turned back briefly to wave to her friends who were still on the school bus. Bright lightning flashed across the sky, streaked through the dark, rolling thunder clouds, and made a loud cracking noise.

She went into the house and put her umbrella into the stand near the door. She took off her shoes and put them on the mat her mother had placed in the entryway.

"Hi, Mom," she called into the house.

"Hello, Dear," her mother called back from the kitchen, just where Frankie knew she would be. It was her baking day. Frankie knew that because the house smelled so wonderful on baking days.

Frankie knew her mother had been in the kitchen most of the day. She only baked on Fridays. She always said it was a chore that she only wanted to face once a week, but the whole family knew she loved cooking and baking. There was no recipe which she would not try.

Frankie went into the kitchen, kissed her mother on the cheek, and took a couple of cookies from the platter on the counter.

"Did you have a good day?" her mother asked.

"Oh, yes," Frankie answered, "it was awesome! I got six new books from the library! Three of them are books about history, two are mysteries, and one is a book about monsters. I'm planning on reading that one first. I'm so excited. I got enough books to keep me busy all weekend. I don't have any homework so I can't wait to get started on them."

Her mother smiled. She knew how much Frankie loved to read. Everybody knew that about her.

"Okay, Sweetheart," she said, "I'll call you when it's time for dinner. I know exactly where you will be."

"That's right," Frankie said excitedly, "I'll be in my room devouring these books. I can hardly wait! Yippee, new books!" she added.

Her mother laughed. "I know how you are when you get your hands on a book that you haven't read. You're even excited when you get the chance to read books you've already read before," she said.

Frankie laughed too. She took a bottle of juice from the refrigerator and went upstairs to her room.

She put the cookies and juice on the bedside table and she hung up her coat on the peg next to the door where her jackets and scarves were hanging. She dumped out her backpack on the bed. She separated the books.

She returned the school books to the backpack and hung it on the peg next to her coat. She changed into her around-the-house clothes and eagerly sat down on the bed.

Frankie had *always* loved reading – she read all the time. Her mother was fond of saying that reading makes you smarter, that it helps you learn to spell words correctly, and it helps you have a good vocabulary.

She looked through the library books. She took the time to read the descriptions of each book inside their front covers. She stacked them up on her night stand in the order that she planned to read them.

While she was looking through the books, she ate the cookies she had gotten from the kitchen and she drank the juice.

Her little sister, Aimee, came in to see what she was doing. Aimee was seven years old. She didn't like to read, but she spent a lot of time in her room with her dolls and toys. She had a delightful imagination. She liked to make up wonderful stories about her dolls and she loved to tell them to the family. She would act out her stories with all the drama she could put into the stories to make them real.

When Aimee left, Frankie selected the top book and started to read. What seemed like a short time, but what must have been more than two hours, she heard her mother calling her down to dinner. She noticed that the room was getting dark with the day fading into the evening. She turned on the lamp beside her bed before going down to eat. She hurried down the stairs, eager to tell her father about the new books she got from the library.

After dinner, Frankie helped her mother wash the dishes and clean up the kitchen. The entire time she babbled on and on happily about what she had read in the first book in just a couple of hours.

It was the book about monsters. She loved all books and history books were her absolute favorite, but she couldn't resist a really good monster book. After they finished in the kitchen, Frankie ran up to her room. She couldn't wait to get back to the book.

Frankie went back to reading. She barely noticed the storm outside. She was aware that the storm was still having a good time out there, but she felt she was having a much better time inside, with her nose and her imagination buried in the monster book.

She was really absorbed in the story. Reading it, she was feeling a little uneasy. It was a good book and she felt that she was 'properly' scared by the story. She loved every minute of it. The good parts gave her goosebumps. That was her favorite part of reading scary stories.

Out of the corner of her eye, Frankie thought she saw something in the hall outside her door. It caught her attention without really registering in her mind. She casually glanced up toward the hallway without really noticing anything. It was just a reaction to the movement that she saw. She did see that the hall was dark, but to her mind, it didn't really mean anything. She continued reading.

After a bit, she again thought she saw something, which made her look up. She could see down the dark hall, but there was nothing there. She thought the whole thing was curious. She figured that the family was most likely downstairs, probably watching television. Frankie continued to read.

Then, once again, she noticed something out of the corner of her eye. She looked up from the book. This was the third time. She didn't see anything, not in her room or down the hall. She started to feel a little creeped out.

"It's just your imagination," she said out loud. "Let's not get carried away here, just because we're reading a scary book."

She looked down the dark hallway. Same old hall as always, she said to herself. She looked around her room. Same old bedroom, nothing's changed, and there's nothing here, she added.

"You're getting spooked by the story in the book," she said out loud. "Don't be so silly."

Frankie went back to reading again. Suddenly, she got the feeling that someone was watching her! She looked up quickly, at the room and at the hall, but she didn't see anything.

She wondered whether she should put the book away for the night. Maybe she should read it during the daytime, she considered. But, it was really good, she argued. No, she decided, she was involved in the story and she was dying to find out what was going to happen. She *had* to keep reading!

She read on for several more minutes. Then, she got the creepy feeling again. It scared her to think that someone could be watching her from nearby. She was nervous. She looked over at her bedroom window. The curtains were still open. She was on the second floor, she reasoned. No one could watch her through a window on the second floor, not unless they could fly.

Fly? That was an idea. *Some* monsters *could* fly. She wondered, could a monster hover outside her window and look in at her? It was a scary thought. She got up and went over to the window. She leaned her face close to the glass and looked out.

It was very dark. The storm was still out there. She waited a moment and when the lightning lit up everything, she looked around the yard. She couldn't see anything that didn't belong. She certainly didn't see anything flying around her window.

Frankie closed the curtains – that made her feel a little better. It was just in case a monster flew into the yard and wanted to hover outside her window, she told herself. He would just be wasting his time because now he couldn't look in. He would have to stop flying around and simply move on up the road before his wings got tired. She smiled at the thought of a monster walking down the road because he flew around too long and his wings got tired.

See, it's nonsense, she said to herself. It's all just silly, stupid nonsense. She tried to shake off the creepy feeling. What was there to be afraid of? She decided that she was scaring herself for no reason.

She went back to reading her book. After only a very few minutes, she thought she heard a sound, something like a voice – talking far away, or maybe it was a giggle, she couldn't be sure.

Frankie was starting to get scared for real. This was just getting a little too spooky for her. She listened closely, but she didn't hear anything else. Imagination, she said to herself. It's supposed to be focused into the book and not out here trying to scare the daylights out of me, as her grandmother usually said about being frightened.

Just as she looked back down at the pages of the book, she heard a slight noise from the hall. She looked up again and she thought she could hear a brushing sound.

Wait! Frankie looked down the dark hallway. She caught her breath sharply. She could see two red eyes at the far end of the hall! It was too dark to make out anything else, but she could see the eyes because they were glowing.

Fierce, glowing, red eyes were moving slowly down the hall toward her room! Frankie was suddenly terrified. A monster ... a real live monster was coming down the hall!

This was *not* her imagination. She was too scared to move. As she watched, the glowing eyes came slowly down the hall. They were coming toward her room! She could hear the brushing of the monster's feet as they dragged along the carpet.

Frankie couldn't think straight for a minute. Her mind was all mixed up. She was confused. What should she do? With the monster out in the hall, her way out of the room was blocked! She wouldn't be able to get out! She wondered, should she get up and shut the door?

She could block the door with something so the monster wouldn't be able to get in. That was a real good idea, she decided, but she was frozen in place. She had read that people freeze and can't move when they get scared, but she had never believed it was possible. How can someone be so scared that they were unable to move? That had been her reasoning. To not be able to move – that hadn't seemed real to her. Well, it sure seemed real now.

She also read that people couldn't scream when they were scared. She never believed that either. She opened her mouth to call out, to ask who was out there, but no sound came out. What she read was obviously true, she decided in the back of her mind.

Frankie felt like she didn't have a choice. Either she had to get up and block the door, or she could just sit there until the monster got to the doorway. At that point she wouldn't be able to shut the door.

She swallowed hard and took a deep breath. She clenched her fists to give her courage. She looked down the hall and she could still see the red glowing eyes. They had stopped halfway down the hall from her room. She decided that now was the perfect time. She jumped up and ran toward the door!

Just as Frankie reached the doorway, the hall lights came on, and the hallway was all lit up. She was confused because she saw Aimee standing there next to the light switch halfway down the hall. It didn't make sense in her mind for a moment.

Aimee was wearing a monster costume and she had a headband on her head. The band had two antenna attached to it and there was a red ball on the end of each antenna. The red balls were lit up from a bulb inside of them.

When Frankie stopped short in the doorway, looking confused, Aimee collapsed into a fit of giggles in the hallway.

"I got you, I got you!" she squealed delightedly between giggles. She was holding her arms across her stomach and rocking back and forth on the floor. "You were scared," she said. "Oh, that was so great! I got you!"

"No," Frankie answered, "I was *not* scared! I knew it was you, you sneaky little trickster."

"No way," Aimee said, "I saw you were scared. This is going to be a really great story."

"No, I knew it all the time. I was just playing along with your little trick," Frankie said.

"I think you were scared," Aimee said again.

"No, I wasn't," Frankie insisted. "That just proves what a great actress I am. You didn't fool me for a minute. No one will believe your story. They'll know it's all made up."

She wasn't about to tell her sister that she was not only scared, but she had actually been terrified. She had a silent conversation with herself: 'Well, let this be a lesson to you, old girl,' she said inside her head. 'When you let your imagination get out of the book you see what can happen?'

'Your little sister dressed in last year's Halloween costume got the better of you! You should have recognized the lighted antenna on her head. You helped her pick out that costume and you even took her trick-or-treating in it.' Frankie felt very relieved, but she didn't dare allow Aimee to see that.

The End

It was a dark and stormy night ...

Gina

There had been thunder and lightning for the past half an hour. Young eight-year-old Gina felt safe under the covers on her bed. She had always been afraid during big storms. Her friends at school told her that they get under the covers when a storm comes with lightning and thunder in it. They were positive that it was the surest and very safest way to make it through a storm. She had decided to give it a try because it worked for her friends. She found out that it was a really good plan. It worked great for her too. Ever since then, she always found her safe shelter under the blankets on her bed.

The storm came along just before bedtime, so she was going to bed anyway. Her father promised her that the storm was moving very fast and it would not last long. Still, she thought it was a good idea to hide under the blanket just in case. It was just like being in a tent. It was like camping out and she liked the feeling that she was safe under there.

Gina decided that if the storm wasn't gone before she fell asleep, then she would just stay under the covers and pretend that she really *was* camping out. She had fallen asleep before without any fear while in her safe tent. She was glad that her friends had such a great idea.

Maybe her father was right. The thunder was starting to sound like a rumble instead of a roar. She had been watching the lightning that she could see through her blanket and counting until the thunder came. It told her how far away the storm was.

Her father had taught her that counting trick. He said that every second that went by between the lightning and the thunder meant that the storm was that many miles away. After she saw the lightning, she counted one thousand one, one thousand two, and so on until the thunder came. The higher she was able to count, the better she felt. She liked the counting idea. It helped her feel better and better, until the storm was completely gone away.

Now, she couldn't see any more lightning, so she wasn't able to count up to the thunder any longer. She decided that the storm had moved far enough away that she didn't need to hide from it.

While Gina was making the decision to come out from under her safe tent, she thought that she heard a growling sound. What could it be, she wondered? At first she couldn't place the sound. She wasn't sure she had heard it before. Well, she thought, maybe it *was* familiar, but she had never heard it in her room before.

She waited and after a minute she heard it again. She believed it sounded like an animal growling. Can that be right, she wondered? Can an animal be in her room? Gina sat up and uncovered her head so she could hear better and she listened closely. After a few minutes she heard it again.

Wait! She thought it sounded like it came from under the bed! There shouldn't be any animals in her room, she said to herself. There *can't* be any animals under the bed, she argued, trying not to be scared at the idea that it might be true.

Gina didn't have any pets. Her twin brother, Greg, had a fish tank in his room and her mother had two canaries in a cage downstairs. None of them could growl, so she decided that it must be her imagination. After a minute or two she heard it again. Oh, no, it *was* under her bed!

Now she was frightened. There was something down there under her bed and it was growling! She looked around the room. It was dark. There weren't any lights on. She couldn't see anything. The door to her room was open, like it always was. The light from the hall was shining in and it gave her some pretty good light, but the room was empty.

Wait! She heard the growling again! Was it louder? She couldn't be sure, but it was clearly down there. She was certain of it now! She knew it was not her imagination. Gina was positive she could hear it coming from under the bed. It must be a monster! How could it get in, she wondered? It could have come in a window, she guessed. Maybe it came down the chimney, downstairs in the living room. It didn't really matter how it got in. The monster got into the house and now it was down under her bed!

Gina started to get out of bed, but she was too afraid to get up. She was worried that, if she put her feet down on the floor, the monster would grab her by the ankles and pull her under the bed. *And she wasn't about to lean over to look under the bed!* That was never going to happen! So, she didn't dare get out of the bed or look under it.

She looked around the room. She was trapped! The growling sounded like it was getting a little louder. The monster must be moving around down under the bed! She decided that she couldn't keep sitting there on the bed. What if the monster came out from under the bed? It might be between her and the door. She wouldn't be able to get away.

Gina sat there trying really hard to figure out what she should do. When she felt she could wait no longer, she considered jumping off the end of the bed and running out into the hallway. Then a different thought stopped her. What if the monster was there, right under the foot of the bed?

No ... she could *not* take a chance like that! There just had to be another way. She leaned a little to her side to look down the hallway. She could see that her parents were still awake. It sounded like they were getting ready for bed in their room down at the end of the hall. Then she had a new idea. She would call her mother!

"Mom," Gina called down the hall. She didn't get an answer. She suddenly realized that, because she was scared, her voice didn't carry very far.

"Mom," Gina yelled louder, "Mom!"

She could hear her mother come rushing down the hall. Her mother stopped just inside the doorway and she flipped on the light switch. The room lit up brightly.

The light made Gina feel better. Just having the light on made everything much better somehow. The light chased away the dark and made her room bright.

"Oh, for goodness sake, what it is, Honey?" her mother asked. "Is something wrong?"

"Mom," Gina almost shouted! "There's a monster under the bed. I can't get up!"

"Honey, there's no monster under the bed," her mother said.

"Sure there is," Gina answered, "because I can hear it growling under there. I'm afraid to get up. I don't want it to grab my feet."

Her mother came farther into the room and she stopped at the foot of the bed. She bent over to look under the bed.

"Mom, be careful," Gina said quietly. She didn't want the monster to hear and know that her mother was going to look under the bed. She was worried the monster would grab her mother and pull her under. Gina held her breath.

Her mother took a quick look under the bed and she stood up. She put her hands on her hips.

"Greg!" she yelled. "Come in here young man!" She pointed to a spot in front of her, like she thought Greg could see her from his room, pointing to the floor in front of her.

"Greg!" she yelled louder.

Greg came out of his room down the hall and came to stand outside Gina's doorway. "What is it, Mom?" he asked.

Gina could tell he was trying to sound innocent. She had heard him use that tone before.

"You know exactly what it is, young man," his mother answered. "Get in here and get that remote control dinosaur out from under Gina's bed and you stop trying to scare your sister!"

"See, Honey," her mother said, as she turned back toward Gina, "there's no monster. It's just your bratty brother trying to be cute."

Gina felt so relieved. Her grandmother was always telling her not to let her imagination get the better of her. Now she knew what Grandma meant.

The End

It was a dark and stormy night ...

Holly

Holly felt like she was worn out. They were doing inventory at work all week and she had been required to stay late every night. She was the supervisor and everyone expected her to be there until the end, just like she had always done when it was inventory time. She was hoping to finish early today because of the storm, but it didn't work out that way.

Driving home in the pouring rain had been a little scary. The bright flashes of the lightning were almost blinding and the loud, cracking thunder made her jump every time it crashed through the sky. Her hands hurt from gripping the steering wheel.

She was glad when she reached the house. She was also glad the inventory at work was all finished and that it was now Friday. Yea! Friday! She smiled to herself. She so looked forward to the weekend. At least she would have a couple of days to relax. A nice, long, quiet weekend sounded better than ice cream. Critter, the big, yellow cat she had rescued from the shelter, met her at the door. He was always there to greet her when she got home. Seeing him at the front door every night made her feel welcomed.

Holly scooped him up, hugged him, and carried him into the bedroom with her. She put him down on the bed and he meowed while she changed clothes. After she got into her pajamas, she scooped him up again and they went into the kitchen together. She fed Critter and cleaned the litter box while he ate.

Then she fed the fish, Georgie and Porgie, and her canary, Pretty Polly. She was almost too tired to eat, but she made herself a quick salad. She ate in the big easy chair in the living room while Critter sprawled across the coffee table, cleaning himself.

After she finished, she and Critter sat together in the big chair and she petted him while she read a book. The storm made the cat nervous and petting him always reassured him. It was a cozy evening.

When she had read a few chapters of the mystery novel she was trying to get through, she was starting to feel sleepy. She covered Pretty Polly's cage for the night.

She turned out all the lights, and went to bed. Critter was already on the bed when she got there.

Holly wasn't sure if she would get much sleep. The storm was still raging outside and, even though the drapes were closed in the bedroom, she could still see the flashes of lightning through them. The booming thunder didn't help either.

In spite of the storm and, probably because she was so tired, she did fall asleep, much quicker than she expected. Of course, Critter didn't seem to have one bit of trouble finding dreamland.

In the middle of the night Holly woke up feeling thirsty. She realized that she had forgotten to put water beside the bed like she usually did. She often got thirsty during the night. She could tell right away that the storm was moving away from the area. The flashes of lightning were much less bright than they had been earlier and the low rumbling of the thunder sounded distant.

She got up and went into the kitchen. She didn't bother to turn on the lights because she knew her way around. She had made that trip to the kitchen many, many times over the years.

She went over to the cabinet, got a glass, and filled it at the sink. While she drank the water, she pulled aside the kitchen curtain above the sink to look out into the backyard. She wanted to check on the storm. She could see that the storm clouds were moving quickly across the sky.

Wait! She suddenly thought she heard a hissing sound behind her. S-s-s-s-s! She froze! She set the glass down on the counter next to the sink and listened closely for the sound, trying to identify it. After a few moments she heard it again. S-s-s-s-s! It was like a soft rattle. Oh, no ... she recognized the sound! It was a snake! It was a RATTLESNAKE!!!!! She was deathly afraid of snakes!

Holly fought back the overpowering urge to scream bloody murder. She didn't want to panic the snake and have it go crazy. She just wanted it to stay put ... wherever it was. She hoped that it wouldn't move. But, a rattlesnake, here in her house – how can that be? How did it get into the house?

Some neighbors mentioned they had seen snakes in the fields out behind the neighborhood and in the forest back there. But, that was a couple of years ago.

She thought someone said the animal control people had cleared them all out. Had new snakes moved in? She hadn't even thought about snakes for a long time. She had walked all through those fields and all around back in the forest too. She hadn't seen anything. Of course, she hadn't been looking either.

S-s-s-s-s! Where was it? She was afraid to move. The snake could be anywhere in the room. Why didn't I turn on the light, she wondered to herself? Well, she answered herself, there wasn't any reason to. How was I to know that I'd need the light?

She stood rooted to the spot, wondering what she should do. Well, I can't just keep standing here, she told herself. She tried to think it out. She had walked straight into the kitchen, so maybe she could just walk straight back out. The light switch was next to the door. She could just turn it on when she reached the doorway.

But, she thought, what if the snake moved across the doorway after I came into the room? I could be walking right up to it. I might even step on it. She felt itchy all over her body with the fright that the thought caused.

She fought back the urge to jump up on the sink counter. That won't do me any good, she said to herself. I'll still have to turn on the light and find that snake. I can't just sit up on the counter until daylight when I can see. Even the morning light might not help. It could be under the edge of the cabinet and I won't know until I put my foot on the floor and zing! It would sink its fangs right into my ankle.

S-s-s-s-s! Holly heard the sound again. Where was it? She turned to face the room with her back against the sink. She tilted her head slightly and listened closely. She would try to pinpoint the sound the next time she heard it. With her ears tuned to any sound, and her eyes staring blindly into the darkness of the room, she stood there for what seemed like forever. She was listening so intently that she could even hear the soft ticking of the kitchen clock on the wall across the room.

S-s-s-s-s! Wait! There it was again! She turned her head to look toward the sound. It came from the direction of the back door. She decided that the next time she heard it, if it was over by the back door, she would cross the room and turn on the light. The back door was probably a good ten feet away.

A snake can't jump that far, can it, she asked herself? She had seen snakes strike on television. It didn't seem like they went very far. Weren't they striking at someone's foot because they stepped next to them? Sure, that was right. They only bite when you nearly step on them. That was their warning to you. And, that rattle, well, that was a warning also – a warning that you were getting too close.

But, how did that snake get into the kitchen, she asked herself? She was frightened at the idea that snakes could just slither into her house at any time. Wouldn't it have to come in through the door?

Holly listened, and again she heard what sounded like a soft rattle from near the back door. She braced herself. She held her breath and then she ran from the kitchen into the living room. She almost collapsed on the sofa but she stopped herself.

If the snake is in the kitchen, I had better get it out while it's trapped in there, she decided. If I wait, it could end up anywhere in the house and I might not be able to find it. It could bite Critter and maybe even eat my Pretty Polly. Poor Pretty Polly ... trapped in her cage. She wouldn't be able to get away.

At least Critter could run, that is, if the snake didn't sneak up on him while he was asleep. She figured Georgie and Porgie would be okay.

Besides, *she* also had to sleep in the house. What about her? The snake could slither up onto the bed and sink its fangs into her at any time. No, she had to do something. The idea of protecting her pets made her feel a little more brave, but she was still terrified.

"I can do this," she said out loud. "I have to. Critter and my Pretty Polly are depending on me to protect them. I can't let anything happen to them."

Wait! She had a thought. Didn't the people on television handle the rattlesnakes with a stick to keep them from biting? Yes, that's right. She remembered that. So ... she could use the broom! That was a good five feet long. She could hold the snake down with it while she opened the back door and then she could sweep it right outside. It sounded like a good plan. Well, it sounded easy, but was it really?

O-o-o-o, she shuddered. Her skin felt creepy. This had to be the scariest thing that she had ever been through, she thought. And probably the bravest thing she had ever considered doing.

She was on her own. There wasn't anyone to help, but she was determined to protect her pets. No matter what, she had to do this, she told herself. It seemed simple. She thought through the steps of her plan: just turn on the light, get the broom, and locate the snake. Then, hold it down with the broom, open the door, and sweep it out! It sounded so easy.

She knew that snake bites were very dangerous and she couldn't take any risky chances. She didn't dare let it roam around the house.

Holly took a deep breath and let it out slowly. She tip toed over to the kitchen doorway. Leaning slightly into the room, she reached her hand around the corner and groped along the wall for the light switch. When she found it, she flipped on the switch and the kitchen was bathed it bright light. She jumped back. She stood still, listening for any sound. Everything seemed quiet in the kitchen.

Then, taking another deep breath, she stepped back up and leaned in through the doorway. She looked around the room. She didn't see the snake. At least it wasn't in the middle of the floor or anywhere that she could see.

S-s-s-s-s! There it was again! Yes, it was definitely over by the door. It sounded like it was behind the kitchen trash can that sat right beside the back door.

She slowly, cautiously, tip toed across the room toward the door. S-s-s-s-s! The sound came again and she almost jumped back. Watching the floor for any sign of movement, she reached out and took the broom off the hook on the wall near the door.

Holly tried to control her breathing. She could hear her heart thumping in her ears. S-s-s-s-s! It sounded like it was down behind the trash can. She reached out and put her hand on the can.

She waited a moment. She took a few breaths, trying to slow down her heart beat. Then, she took hold of the edge of the can and slowly, oh, so slowly, she dragged it away from the wall. S-s-s-s-s! The rattling sound was much louder than it had been. She jumped back! She held the broom out in front of her. She had disturbed it! But, it didn't slither out. She let out her breath.

She leaned forward to look around the can, trying to see behind it. She couldn't see the snake. Maybe it was curled up in the corner back there, she thought.

She took a step closer and leaned a little more so she could see into the corner behind the can. No snake … h-m-m-m, no snake? She was puzzled. She was certain the sound came from here and she was positive the snake hadn't gotten away.

S-s-s-s-s! Oh, it was in the can! She shuddered at the thought that she had just had her hand on that can. She could hear the rattling from inside the can. Somehow it was trapped inside the can! Should she dare pick up the can and throw it out the door?

No, not good, she told herself. She had to find that snake and make sure it was in there. She stood a little way back from the can. Shaking, she slowly turned the broom upside down and held the handle toward the trash can. She took a cautious step forward and gingerly pushed the broom handle into the trash can. Suddenly there was a big rush of sound! S-s-s-s-s-s-s-s-s-s-s-s!!!

She jumped back quickly and dropped the broom. She almost had a heart attack and a squeal escaped from her throat. She was trembling.

Wait! Wait. Wait just a minute, she told herself. She suddenly recognized the sound.

It wasn't a snake after all. She felt so stupid. She realized that earlier she had emptied Critter's litter box into the trash can. She had poured the litter on top of some papers and the sound was the litter sliding off the paper into the bottom of the can. It was just cat litter sliding off the papers! She was so relieved. But, she still felt stupid. How could she have scared herself like that? The sound should have been obvious to her, she thought. She had been hearing it for two years, ever since Critter came home with her.

It must be the storm and all the hours she had been working, she decided. She was so tired that her brain hadn't recognized a familiar sound like that. Maybe it was that mystery book she was reading "That was dumb," she said out loud. "Dumb!"

She took a deep breath and let it out. She straightened up and lifted her shoulders. She picked up the broom and stood it in the corner, turned out the kitchen light, and marched back to bed, knowing that Critter would still be curled up in there having a good night's sleep.

The End

It was a dark and stormy night ...

Ivy Towne

Ivy Towne – she just loved her name. The name sounded like it belonged to a really cool person, and it also sounded like it was a wonderful place too. She liked that.

She loved writing her name and dreaming of the beautiful place it represented. She would write her name in every kind of script she came across. There were papers taped to the wall of her room that had her name written all kinds of ways ... with flowers entwined with the letters, or little elves and fairies peeking around the letters. That's what she was doing ... lying on her bed and writing out her name. She was adding clovers with the letters this time.

"Wait! Did you hear that?" Ivy said into the empty room. She acted like she was talking to someone, but there wasn't anyone there to hear her. She was by herself. She knew that she was all alone. Everyone was gone. The house was empty.

A series of storms had been passing through the area, which had kept everyone inside for days and days. The family was going stir crazy cooped up inside and they were anxious to get out of the house.

Her father called it 'cabin fever' and it seemed like he was right. Everyone was getting grouchy and short-tempered. He said that it surely was symptoms of the fever.

Her mother decided that they had to get out of the house. The whole family went into town to have dinner and see a movie. Ivy wasn't feeling well so she stayed home.

After all, she *was* thirteen now. She was quite capable of staying home alone, she had assured herself. "No, I'm not afraid," she had said to her mother. "Why should I be afraid? There's nothing to be scared of."

"Honey, are you sure?" her mother had asked. "I'll stay home with you if you need me to."

"Mom, stop treating me like a baby," she answered. "I'm practically grown. I think I can stay here for a couple of hours without freaking out. Don't worry about me."

"Okay, Dear, if you're really sure," her mother said, but she sounded a little doubtful. "Ivy Towne ... practically grown," she added, waving her hand in front of her. There was wonder in her voice. "Thirteen is nowhere near practically grown, but if you feel like you'll be all right, then it's settled." She smiled and Ivy knew that her mother was acting out what she was saying and that she was teasing her.

"Mom, I'll just be here in my room. I'll probably be sleeping," Ivy declared, and she had tried hard to sound convincing. "I'm just going to stay right here, that's all. You'll probably be back before I even wake up. I promise you that I will be all right. Don't worry about it, okay?"

"All right, then," her mother said. "If you're certain, then we'll just go on. We won't be gone that long. We'll be back by eleven o'clock. You have my cell number if you need me. And your Aunt Penny lives right down the road. You can always call her and she'll come right over. She can be here within about four minutes."

"Mom," Ivy said, and her voice sounded a bit annoyed, "really?"

"Okay, Honey," her mother had said. She put her hand on Ivy's forehead to reassure herself that her daughter's fever wasn't too high. She looked closely at Ivy's face for a moment or two. She shook her head that she was satisfied and she went to the doorway. She looked back, blew Ivy a quick kiss, and pulled the door almost closed behind her as she left the room.

Ivy could hear her footsteps on the creaky boards of the hallway as she walked away. She could also hear her going down the stairs. Every step squeaked loudly when someone stepped on it. It had always been easy to count the steps, there were twenty-four. She had counted them many, many times over the years. Counting the steps had almost become automatic when someone went up or down the stairway.

The big, old, two-story farm house had always made noises. It had been built over a hundred years ago, but Ivy loved the 'kind of run-down' house, as her father described it. Ivy had lived there her whole life. She could only imagine what it would be like to live somewhere else.

She had always felt comforted by the noises the house made: the creaking floor boards, the squeaking stairs, the little groans the house made when the weather changed from warm to cold and back to warm, and the swooshing noises from the attic above Ivy's room when it was windy outside.

She even liked the soft screech of the rooster weather vane on top of the house that turned in the wind. You couldn't always hear it, but when the wind was strong it was louder.

All of the sounds were familiar to her. She felt kind of soothed by the sighs and the grumbles the house made when it was 'settling' as her father explained it; somehow it always made her feel safe. It was very pleasant.

The big, old house was like an old friend. Knowing the house was settling down at night made her feel happy as she settled down herself in her room every evening.

Ivy could hear the rain as it pinged against the panes of the window in her room and she could hear the blowing wind swooshing through the attic above her head.

She wasn't sure if she would be able to hear the familiar sounds of the house over all the racket the storm was making outside. But, she felt warm and comfortable snuggled down under the comforter on her bed, printing her name in different colors on her sketch pad.

Wait! A board squeaked! Ivy was surprised. She sat up in her bed and listened closely. Was it just the house settling, was it the storm, or was it a footstep? She couldn't decide. Oh, there it was again! It can't be the house, she figured. It seemed like it was too loud to be the house. It sounded like a footstep!

The house wouldn't make the same noise twice inside of a minute, Ivy told herself. Would it? She wondered about that. She heard it again. Then, it sounded again, only louder. It was the stairs!

It definitely had to be footsteps ... but, how could anyone get in, she asked herself? I just know they locked the door when they left. Well, she didn't really *know* that. Could they have forgotten to lock the door? No ... her mother was concerned about leaving her there alone. She *certainly* wouldn't forget to lock the door ... right?

Ivy felt a little better thinking that her mother would never forget to lock the door. She would want her to be safe. Besides, no one had ever come into the house, not ever, not once in all these years. So, why would someone come in tonight, on the only night when she was here alone? No, it didn't make any sense, she thought. It was crazy.

Squeak! Squeak! Oh, no, it's the stairs all right! Someone's coming up! She knew the familiar sound of the steps. It was certainly the stairs!

Ivy was really nervous. No ... she was scared! She realized that she was *really* scared. "Why did everybody leave me here alone?" she whispered to herself. "Just because I was sick, they didn't have to all go off to the movies. Someone could have stayed here with me."

She scolded herself, "You're the one who told them to go without you. It was your own idea. Don't blame them for going."

"Pull yourself together," she said quietly and sternly to herself. "You're thirteen years old! Don't start acting like a baby. You're practically grown, remember?"

Besides, what would people say, she thought? *Well,* she argued against the thought, people don't have a prowler coming up their stairway! She felt her heart beating. It felt like it was climbing up in her chest. It was beating so fast that it was making it hard for her to breathe. She tried to calm down. She had to keep thinking clearly.

We don't have anything of value here, she thought. What could anyone possibly want? Do they want to take the television set?

Suddenly, a new thought occurred to her. If I see him I'll be a witness. What do they say on those television shows, something about not leaving any witnesses behind? I could be in real trouble! No, I won't be in trouble because I might die of fright long before he can see me.

Ivy was more than scared now, a lot more! She was terrified. Crazy thoughts were running through her head. Why do we have to live out here at the edge of town where there's no one near? Why do we have to live so far off the road that no one can hear me scream? Why do we have to live in this old run-down house with floors that squeak at the slightest touch?

Why hadn't she just gone to the movies? Why, why? What in the world made her want to stay home alone? She must be crazy! She felt her lips shaking with fear. She pressed them together to stop them.

Was that another footstep? She couldn't hear very well because her heart was pounding like a drum in her ears. I wish they would hurry and come back from the movies, she thought. They'll probably come in late and find me in my bed, dead of fright. They'll be able to see the terror on my face.

There! She heard another step! She could hear the creak of the floor board in the hall outside the door. Ivy felt dizzy. She felt frozen. She couldn't move. She felt like she couldn't get up. She didn't think she could even yell for help. No one would hear her anyway, except whoever was in the hall outside the door. That would surely frighten him and he would know that she was there.

Wait! The footsteps stopped! And her heart almost stopped too! Look, she said to herself, her mother left the door cracked open a tiny bit. She could see the light from the hall, but not anyone standing there. Shouldn't there be a shadow, she reasoned?

Then, there was silence outside the door. Maybe this is all just my imagination, she thought. That idea made her feel a little better. She took a deep breath and let it out slowly. I have *got* to get up, she said to herself. She was upset with herself for being so afraid. This was something she had to do – something that she would have to handle for herself. She never considered herself to be brave, but there had never been a situation where she had to be brave.

Ivy scooted over to the edge of the bed. I've got to go and see who's there, she told herself. I don't want to get trapped in this room. Don't be so scared, she said. All I have to do is grab the door and swing it open. Maybe I can run past whoever is out there. If I'm lucky I can get away. I can run down the stairs and out the front door.

I can run to the Mitchell's house, she decided. It's not far. I know you can see their house across the field from here. They'll be awake. They'll let me in. Yeah, that's a good plan, she believed. That's what I have to do. You've *got* to be brave, she told herself, and she tried to sound forceful to bolster her courage. Just take a deep breath and go.

Okay, she decided, there was no other choice here. She *had* to do this and she was *determined* to do it. Ivy braced herself. She was ready to go. She got up and quietly crept across the room to the door. She reached out and took hold of the door knob! She held her breath. 1, 2, 3 GO! She swung the door open! There was a large, shadowy figure in the hall! They were blocking her way! She started to run but she ran right into the figure!

The shadowy person quickly grabbed her by the shoulders and held her so she wouldn't fall and she couldn't get away. Ivy screamed.

"Oh, my goodness!" the figure exclaimed.

Ivy realized that her eyes were tightly closed. She slowly opened them. She looked up and saw that it was her Aunt Penny. She almost fainted with relief when she realized it wasn't a stranger.

"Oh, you scared me to death!" Ivy breathed. "What are you doing here? I thought someone broke into the house! Why were you sneaking through the house?"

"Oh, Ivy, Honey, I didn't mean to scare you," Aunt Penny answered. "Are you okay?"

"You know, I almost had a heart attack!" Ivy said, clutching her chest in a dramatic gesture. "I almost died of fright."

"I'm sorry, Sweetie," Aunt Penny answered. "Your mother said that you'd be asleep and I didn't want to wake you up. I was just going to take a quick peek and then go."

"But, how'd you get in here?" Ivy asked.

"I saw your folks in town. Your mother said you stayed home sick. She knew that I'd be passing the house on my way home. Because of the storm, she asked me to stop and check on you. I have my own key so I let myself in. I intended to look in on you and leave, that's all."

"Oh, my," Ivy said. "I've never been so scared in my life."

"Well, you're okay now," Aunt Penny answered.

The End

It was a dark and stormy night ...

Jessie

Jessie was on the way to the family cabin. She was looking forward to being up at the lake. The family hadn't been there since last summer. They never went up there in the winter because of the snow. Sometimes it snowed a lot in the mountains and it wasn't easy to get to the lake. But, now that it was spring, they were excited about going there, especially after being cooped up inside all winter.

Last night had been a really, really stormy night. The thunder and the lightning were bad enough, but the wind and the rain made it a terrible storm. Jessie had never liked storms. They scared her.

The storm had put a damper on their plans to go up to the cabin for the weekend and they were feeling a little disappointed. Her father checked the weather and he said that the lake was three hours away and there was no rain storm there. Jessie felt that it would be a nice weekend without the thunder and lightning waking her up at all hours of the night.

Her older sister, Regina, and her little brother, Mickey, were also looking forward to getting away. They always had a lot of fun at the lake. They could wander around in the forest that surrounded the lake and they could go out on the water. Her father always went fishing. That was his favorite thing to do at the lake. Her mother loved to sit on the dock and soak up the sunshine while the kids swam and floated around in the water.

Jessie leaned forward from the back seat of the car to see out the front windshield. She was eager to see the end of the dark clouds they were driving under. She wanted to see the sunshine that would be streaming down in wonderful-looking sun rays to light up the road ahead. After a while she could see a break in the darkness on the road in front of the car. She watched as the clouds came to an end and they drove out into the sunshine. Hello spring, she said silently. She was happy.

When they reached the cabin, they all helped unload the car and carry the stuff inside. They had a big ice chest her father always brought along. They couldn't lift it, so he was the one who had to carry it up the steps to the front door and into the cabin.

Since it was late afternoon when they reached the cabin, they decided they would wait until the next day to go out onto the water. Jessie's mother had a great idea though. She suggested that they build a fire on the little beach next to their dock and have a cookout down by the water.

Hot dogs and chili dogs were always a big hit on the beach. The kids loved cooking out down there. After they finished off the hot dogs, they made s'mores out of graham crackers, little chocolate squares, and marshmallows.

Jessie loved to roast marshmallows on the end of a stick. She had learned that at summer camp a few years before and she made sure the marshmallows were packed when they were heading to the cabin. They sat around the fire and sang songs while they ate and then their father told a couple of ghost stories. They had a great time.

They were all tired, so they put out the fire and went to bed. Jessie slept so soundly in the quiet of the forest that she didn't wake up until she smelled bacon cooking in the kitchen. She saw that Regina was already gone from their room and she wondered why she hadn't heard her get up and leave.

After breakfast, Jessie and Regina went for a walk in the forest. Their mother didn't want them to go into the water until a little later when the sun had had a chance to warm up the water a little. So they decided to walk through the forest to the marina down the way and then walk back up the road to the cabin. They loved how the forest was turning green.

The sisters walked through the trees, picking and smelling the new flowers that were growing at the foot of the trees and all over the ground. Jessie decided that it would be a beautiful spring and that would bring a great summer. Maybe when they came back in the summer she would bring a couple of her friends to have fun with.

Sometimes her parents would invite other families they were friends with to come up. The families would come up for a weekend, or for a few days, and then go back home while Jessie's family stayed at the lake. If her father had to go back to work in the city, her mother would stay at the lake with the kids and sometimes her sister would come for a visit. Her Aunt Grace lived over on the east coast so the sisters didn't see each other that often and she loved visiting, especially when they were staying up at the lake.

Besides, it gave Jessie's mother someone to talk to while her husband was away at work during the week. He would come up on the weekends during the summer when they were there for a couple of weeks. Sometimes they would go to the lake for two or three weeks at the beginning of summer and then go again for a couple of weeks at the end of summer before school started.

In the afternoon the kids went down to the dock with their mother. She set up her lounge chair, put on her straw hat, and settled down in the sunshine with a book. Her father had been gone all day – fishing since early morning. He always said that was the best time to catch the fish ... before they woke up enough to be aware of what was happening. His idea must have been good because he always came back with a bunch of fish.

The girls went swimming while Mickey floated around on his inner tube. His inner tube had a long rope tied onto it and the other end was tied to the dock so Mickey couldn't float away on the current of the lake. He could have a good time out there without his mother worrying that he had drifted off and gotten into trouble.

After they got tired of swimming, they all went back to the cabin so their mother could start dinner. Jessie turned back to have a look at the lake. The afternoon sun was low in the sky and she loved the way it would shine on the water and make it light up and sparkle.

Jessie told Regina that she would take their swim suits and hang them up to dry on the rack in the bathroom. She gathered the suits and went into the back of the cabin. As she was arranging the suits on the rack, she noticed a movement from the window.

She looked over at the window and she could see a shadow on the outside of the window shade. She looked at it curiously for a minute. She couldn't place the shadow in her mind. But, it looked like someone was outside the window. It was a funny idea. It was a strange shadow. It was a weird shape. The shadow had spiky hair. She wondered how someone outside could reflect on the window shade. She knew the cabin was built several feet above the ground. She thought that someone would have to be kind of tall to cast a shadow on the window. She stood there, looking at the shadow. She wondered if she should look out the window to see who it was.

As Jessie looked at the shadow it moved slightly. She jumped. Wait! She suddenly sorted out what was in her head. She thought she might know what the shadow was – it was tall ... with spiky hair ... oh, my goodness, she realized – it was BIGFOOT!

She thought about her conclusion. Then, she finally grasped what was running through her mind. Bigfoot was outside the window, casting a shadow on the shade! The sun going down over the lake was behind Bigfoot and it was making the shadow. He was right outside!

She was scared. She stooped down so she wasn't level with the window. She was too scared to run past the window to the door. She got down on the floor between the sink counter and the wall and she hid.

She waited and she held her breath, hoping that the Bigfoot would go away, but it stayed there. She had seen the shows on television where people talked about how scared they were when they ran into Bigfoot in the forest. Her family had been coming to the cabin all her life and none of them had ever seen Bigfoot. She guessed that they had never worried about it because they had never seen it and it never crossed Jessie's mind that she would *ever* see it.

She crouched down out of sight, waiting and waiting, but the Bigfoot stood there! She was afraid to move. If he saw her, he might break the window and grab her. She could scream all she wanted but, by the time someone got there, the Bigfoot would be long gone, carrying her away into the forest where they might never find her.

She could feel herself shaking. She wasn't cold, so she knew it was because she was scared. Suddenly, Regina came into the room and stopped.

"You didn't come back, so I came looking for you," she said.

"Sh-h-h-h," Jessie hissed, holding her finger up to her lips.

Regina asked, "What is it? What are you doing down there?"

"Sh-h-h-h," Jessie said again. She pointed at the window and whispered urgently, "Bigfoot!"

Regina turned and looked at the window. Jessie saw her eyes widen with surprise. Then, she looked scared and she ducked down next to Jessie between the sink counter and the wall! The two girls sat for a few minutes without talking. They just stared at the window.

Regina leaned close to Jessie and whispered, "How do you know it's Bigfoot?"

"Look at it," Jessie whispered back. "See the hair? See how tall it is? The window is probably ten feet from the ground. What else is that tall?"

"It might be a bear," Regina suggested. "They're kind of tall."

"Not *that* tall," Jessie replied. "They don't stand up straight to make them really tall do they?"

"You're right," Regina agreed quietly. "It must be Bigfoot! What does he want? Maybe we should make a run for it."

Jessie shook her head and said, "If we get up and he sees us, he might break in and grab us."

"Oh, that's really scary," Regina said, and she looked scared too.

As the girls were whispering and trying to decide what to do, their mother came into the room.

"My word," she exclaimed, "what on earth are you two doing down there on the floor. Is it a game? Are you playing hide and seek with Mickey?"

"Sh-h-h-h," Jessie shushed. "We're scared."

Her mother asked, "What is there to be afraid of in here?"

Regina pointed at the window. "Bigfoot's out there," she explained. "You can see his shadow on the shade. We're afraid he'll catch us if we get up."

Their mother turned and looked at the window. She stood there for a minute, just staring at the window. The sisters watched her. She didn't even seem afraid. Then, she stepped over to the window.

"Mom, wait!" Jessie hissed. "Don't look out there!"

Her mother ignored her warning. She lifted the corner of the shade and peeked outside. She turned back to the girls and said, "It's all right. There's nothing to worry about. There's no Bigfoot out here."

"But we can see his shadow right there on the shade," Jessie insisted.

"No, get up and come have a look," her mother answered. She held onto the bottom of the shade. She pulled it down and then raised it to the top of the window. "Come on, see for yourselves."

The girls got up and cautiously approached the window. They held onto each other for safety while they turned slowly toward the window. They leaned forward together. They were afraid to look, but their mother didn't seem afraid.

As they looked out, their mother said, "See, there's your Bigfoot." She pointed out the window. "It's just a porcupine. He must have climbed up that tree that's leaning over outside the window. The sun behind him put his shadow on the shade."

"Oh," the girls said at the same time.

"There's no Bigfoot around here," their mother added. "My goodness, you've been up here hundreds of times and have you ever seen a Bigfoot, or even a bear, or a cougar, or anything?"

"No," they had to admit.

"There *are* forest creatures, but they don't come into the areas where people are living, not unless someone leaves food out and they're hungry," she said. "There's nothing to worry about. Your father's back and dinner's ready." She pulled down the shade and the girls followed her out of the room. They were relieved, but they felt silly that they were too afraid to look and see what was making the shadow.

Jessie decided that next time she would be brave enough to look instead of scaring herself.

The End

It was a dark and stormy night ...

Keena

Keena got off the school bus with his best friend. He and Justin left the paved road where the bus let them off and walked down the narrow road that led to Justin's house.

They lived in a long, narrow valley. The valley was mostly dairy farms and just about everyone had built their houses a distance from the main road. Little dirt and gravel roads led to the farms from the paved main road.

Keena lived about two miles farther down the road from where Justin got off the bus. But, today, he got off with Justin because they planned to practice their quick starts for track because they had a really big track meet coming up the following Friday. They were hoping to win their events at the upcoming meet because it would qualify them for the state meet in just a couple of weeks. They were the two best sprinters on the track team.

They had borrowed the team's start clapper from Andrew, the assistant coach who worked with the sprinters on getting out of the starting blocks quickly when the gun went off to start a race. The clapper was two blocks connected together on one end so you could open them and then 'clap' them back together. The clap of the two blocks mimicked the sound of the starter's gun so they could practice at home over the weekend.

It had been raining for most of the day. A big storm had blown in two days before and, although they hadn't had the thunder and lightning today, the weatherman on television said the next wave of the storm was expected overnight.

The two boys talked about the storm and all the rain they had gotten recently. They hoped the series of springtime storms would be over in time for the state track meet.

They wanted to practice at school, but they didn't want to miss the school bus. If they stayed for practice, they would have missed the bus and they would have had to wait for someone to come into town and pick them up.

Usually, they caught a ride with Bryan's dad. His dad owned the hardware store so he was still in town when track practice ended. Bryan was also on the team but he was sick and hadn't been at school for the past two days.

Keena's and Justin's families were dairy farmers and the boys knew that everyone would be busy with the afternoon milking time. It wouldn't be so easy for someone to break away and come into town and get them from school.

On Justin's farm there was an old stable from back when his grandfather kept horses. In front of the stalls, the whole length of the stable was covered by a roof so they could practice on cement instead of dirt and they could stay dry at the same time.

The boys stopped at the house, changed clothes, and got a quick snack. They went out to the stable and practiced their starts along the front of the old stable. After a while Keena noticed that it seemed to be getting darker out than it should be. He looked up at the sky and he could see the dark, heavy, black clouds rolling slowly along in the distance, heading toward them.

Keena figured that he should leave soon before the storm reached the area. That would give him time to reach home before it rained.

The boys agreed that they'd had enough for the day. They decided that they would get together on Saturday and Sunday afternoons, after they finished their chores around their farms.

They gathered up their equipment and headed back to the house. While Keena changed his clothes, Justin said that he would put Keena's stuff in his backpack. While they were talking, they heard a crack of lightning and a boom of thunder coming from a distance.

Keena realized that the storm might be closer than they figured. He believed he could walk home in maybe thirty minutes. He had walked the distance thousands of times. Well, he thought, maybe it wasn't exactly *that* many, but it had been a lot of times over the years. He smiled to himself over the thought.

Heck, it was only two miles up the road, he said to himself. He was used to walking it. It wasn't like he hadn't walked it in the rain before … no big deal. But, he knew he needed to leave right away.

Justin held up his backpack for him and Keena turned around and slipped into it. They went out onto the porch. Justin asked if he was sure he wanted to walk home. He said that, if he waited until after the milking was done, his dad would surely give him a lift.

"No, it's okay," Keena answered. "It's cool – it ain't no big deal – just a little rain."

"All right, then," Justin said. "Go for it! You can always run." He grinned at his own joke.

Keena laughed. "No, I think I've had just about enough running for the day. It's nothing. I'm sure I can get home before the storm gets here. Besides, I've got some homework to do."

"You can do your homework here," Justin offered.

"Nah," Keena answered, "I left the rough drafts and the research stuff for the papers I'm working on at home. I'll have to be there to work on them."

They both looked toward the horizon in the direction of the storm. The dark clouds were just about to swallow up the sun that was already low in the sky. Keena left the porch and started up the road. He turned to wave at Justin.

"See you tomorrow," Justin called, as he waved back. "Call me." He turned and went into the house.

Keena saw a couple of raindrops plinking in the puddles along the road that led up to Justin's house, but he wasn't worried about the rain at that point. He reached the main road and turned in the direction of his farm. He started walking along the shoulder of the road.

Suddenly, there was a flash of lightning, followed by a loud clap of thunder! It surprised him and made him jump. It seemed to be really close. The storm was moving over the fields and the dark clouds had covered the sun. Now, it seemed just like nighttime out there on the road.

Being out in the dark didn't worry him. He knew where he was going. Out on the country road there weren't any street lights, of course, but he knew the landmarks and he was very familiar with the lights he could see at the farmhouses he passed. The houses were a ways back from the main road, but he could see the lights twinkling in the yards around them as he passed the little roads leading up to them. It was a comforting sight.

There were trees along some parts of the road, like narrow strips of forest running along both sides. His father said they were planted many years ago to serve as a windbreak for the winds that blew snow across the valley in the winter. The farmers hoped the trees and fences would catch some of the snow and have it pile up against them instead of settling across the fields making it more difficult to get around in the wintertime months.

The rest of the year the trees and fences kept the winds and the dust down to a minimum, so the herds could wander about and graze across the fields without having to deal with the weather so much.

After a second flash of lightning and another crack of thunder, Keena decided that he should hurry. He started walking a little faster. As he walked along, he thought he could make out the sound of a horse on the road behind him.

The horse didn't seem to be in a hurry. It sounded like it was just walking along. It was curious, but he didn't pay much attention to it at first. As Keena walked it seemed to get a little louder. He wondered how it could catch up when it was walking slowly.

Keena turned around and walked backwards for a few steps so he could look down the road behind him. He couldn't see anything back there. Of course now it was too dark to see very far anyway. He waited for the next flash of lightning to light up the road so he could see farther.

After the lightning flash, he still didn't see anything behind him. Besides, he told himself, no one would be riding their horse in this weather. The storm would spook the horse and it would be really hard to handle. He must have imagined it, he decided. He kept walking.

A quick flash of lightning over his head startled him and he jumped at the suddenness of it. Then, a really super-loud thunder clap tried to burst his eardrums. Whoa ... his ears were ringing. He knew that the rain would be coming along soon. He decided that he should walk faster.

He quickened his pace. After the thunder rolled away and was grumbling in the distance, he thought he heard the sound of the horse on the road behind him again. He walked a little faster and the clip clop of the horse's hooves on the road speeded up also.

He glanced back over his shoulder, but he still couldn't see anyone or anything behind him on the road. He was starting to feel a little nervous. He walked a little faster and, again, the clip clop behind him got faster too.

Then, he started to feel a little afraid, thinking that someone on a horse might be coming up behind him in the dark without seeing him. It was especially unsettling that he couldn't see anyone back there, but he could definitely hear them.

Keena started to move at a slow jog. The clip clop picked up too! *Now*, he was getting scared. He had gone from nervous to afraid to scared. What the heck, he said to himself. This wasn't like him. What's going on? Was there such a thing as an invisible horse?

Wait! Wait a minute, he told himself. He had read that story, the one about a headless horseman. He wasn't seen either, until he was ready to swing his sword at someone. Now that he thought about it, he believed the story took place somewhere that wasn't too far from the area where he lived. He thought he remembered something from the story, something that told where it happened.

Yeah, right, and that *somewhere* wasn't that far away from here, he decided. His brother told him it was just a story that somebody made up, but he wasn't so sure. He had seen a show on television about urban legends. People thought that they were made-up stories, but on the show they talked about the legends having a basis in fact. Their roots were true stories that really did happen and they got distorted in the telling and retelling, but they were really true.

The clip clop behind him was getting louder! Did that mean they were getting closer? Keena picked up the pace of his jog. It was getting closer to a run rather than a jog. The clip clop behind him got louder. His heart was starting to pound. He could feel the fear creeping up his body.

He shouldn't have thought about that urban legend stuff, he decided. It was making him feel creepy. He was scaring himself for no reason. No, that clip clop behind him was what was scaring him and he definitely wasn't imagining it. He couldn't blame it on his imagination. It was there all right. He took a quick glance back. No one ... he couldn't see anyone back there.

Clip Clop! The sounds were louder and faster. He was absolutely positive that he wasn't imagining it. There was definitely a horse on the road behind him. What else sounded like that? There was nothing that he could think of. He started to run. Maybe he would make it to his road before the horse could catch up. He ran faster ... Clip Clop, Clip Clop ... the hooves on the pavement were overtaking him!

"Leave me alone!" Keena shouted back over his shoulder. "Get out of here! Leave me alone!" His voice sounded squeaky. He was really scared now. He was starting to panic!

The faster he ran, the faster the hoof beats became. They were gaining on him. He felt like he couldn't run any faster. He was certain he couldn't outrun a horse! He was beginning to think that he wouldn't be able to make it to his road.

He was running as fast as he could! He was winded. He could feel a pain in his side. No ... it didn't look like he was going to make it.

CLIP CLOP! CLIP CLOP! He was starting to feel dizzy! He was really getting desperate! Was it a maniac? Was someone trying to scare him?

He felt like he was about to drop dead ... right there in the middle of the road! He determined that he couldn't go any farther. His body was going to give out. His heart just couldn't take any more.

So, Keena made a decision. He would just stop. Maybe, whoever was behind him would simply pass on by. But, surely they could see him racing along the road, right? Why were they going faster and faster when he went faster?

He decided that if it was some kind of crazy lunatic, then they would just have to get him. He would have to surrender because this run was done! This decision was life-changing ... maybe even life-ending! But, it was settled ... he would give in. The notion made him feel strangely calm. He accepted the idea. The headless horseman would catch up because he didn't seem to be able to outrun the monster.

At the point where he felt like he just couldn't make it one more step, and his lungs felt like they were about to burst, he slowed down. He saw a patch of grass along the side of the road up ahead. When he got there, he threw himself face down in the grass and covered his head with his arms.

After a moment or two, he realized that everything was quiet. Keena waited. Nothing happened. He could no longer hear the horse. He looked up and peered into the darkness down the road. He couldn't see anyone and he was sure that he hadn't heard them pass. If they had gone by him, then he would have heard the hoof beats fading down the road, right? Nothing ... he sat up and looked up and down the road. No, nothing. He was alone on the road. That was weird, he said to himself. What the heck?

He took off his backpack so he could catch his breath. He sat the backpack beside him in the grass. As he sat it down, he heard a little clapping sound. It seemed weird. He took a closer look at his backpack. He had to laugh. He laughed out loud! It was a huge laugh of relief. He shook his head.

Keena quickly realized what happened. When Justin put his track shoes in the backpack, he had hung the starter clapper on the outside of the pack instead of putting it inside. Maybe he couldn't fit it in there so he just stuck it on the back. Why hadn't he noticed that? Oh, yeah, Justin had held up the pack and he had just slipped his arms through. He never saw the rear of the pack.

He reached out and flipped the clapper a couple a couple of times. Clip clop! That was the sound the two pieces of wood made when they hit together twice. He realized that, as he had hurried along the road, the clapper was bouncing on the rear of the backpack. With every bounce the clapper opened and closed. It sounded just like a horse's hooves. Darn that Justin! His best friend had almost killed him – making him run like that! He could have dropped dead out here – and he almost did! Well, didn't he? It was close, he answered himself.

Keena smiled. He was so relieved. He understood what happened. Justin probably didn't think about it. He just stuck the clapper on the backpack. What difference did it make? Keena didn't make the connection because he never saw it. "What a ding dong," he said into the darkness. He was scared for nothing. He made a promise to himself that he would never, not ever, mention this to Justin, not in a million years.

The End

It was a dark and stormy night ...

Logan

"Boy is it dark!" Logan said aloud. He had pulled his car over to the side of the narrow country road. He looked out at the trees along the road. They grew right up to the edge and went down both sides as far as he could see. It looked like a long, dark hallway.

It was a gloomy, rainy night. Mist had begun to form in the trees and float across the road. It was spooky being out here alone on the deserted road.

He had been to visit his grandparents. They lived out in the country on their farm. He always went out to help his grandfather when he needed extra help. Since it was so late, they had advised him to just spend the night and go home in the morning. Well, he *was* tired from helping around the farm all day. But, since he had football practice in the morning, he decided that he should just go on home. He hoped he could get a few hours of sleep before he had to get up and go to practice.

He was driving along listening to the radio to keep himself awake. He figured he would be home in an hour or so. He was looking forward to lying down in his own bed. The sight of his bed would be a *very* welcome sight. Then, as he was driving along, the car engine suddenly began to sputter. He looked down at the dashboard lights and saw that the fuel gauge was on empty.

Dang it! He was angry with himself. He had passed a service station out near the farm earlier. It was still open when he went by tonight. He had argued with himself about whether he should stop for gas. He decided that he could make it into town and save himself the time it would take to stop.

Now, he really regretted that decision. It would have only taken a few minutes to stop but he was in such a hurry to get home that he had decided to push on.

The route home was a long, narrow country road through thick forest. Hardly any people lived along the road. It was like being in the middle of nowhere. Now it was one o'clock in the morning and he realized he had made a huge mistake.

When the engine died he had coasted over to the narrow shoulder of the road so he would be out of traffic in case someone came along. After he stopped and switched off the headlights, he saw how very dark it was. It was pitch black. Because of the stormy weather and dark clouds, there was no moon. It was like being in a scary movie.

He had been sitting in the car for almost two hours, out in the dark. The rain had continued from time to time. The mist in the trees had gotten thicker and turned into fog. The dense fog was making everything look spookier than ever. No cars had passed in all the time he had been sitting there.

He wasn't sure of what he should do, but he was getting *really* tired of just sitting there. He had been checking his cell phone ever so often. He looked at it again – ugh, still no service. It had always been hard to get service out in the area because of all the trees.

What to do? Should he continue to sit in the car – that wasn't his favorite option? Or, should he get out and walk until he could get a signal on his phone and call his parents, or he could even keep walking until he reached town?

Since the car wouldn't run, there was no heat and he was getting chilly just sitting there. He knew he should not have taken out those two blankets that he usually kept in the back seat. But, he needed the space for his friends when they went bowling a couple of weeks back. He could have just put them in the trunk. That would have been the smart thing to do but, he was cleaning out the car to make space and he had just taken everything into the garage and left them there.

Well, he thought, what should he do? He was *so* tired of sitting there. He was kind of an impatient person and the waiting was driving him crazy. And he was tired of scolding himself for not stopping for gas.

He had already called himself idiot, lunk head, stupid, ding dong, dense, and lazy fool. He had added buffoon, dimwit, thick-headed dummy, and every other name he could think of for making the brainless, rash, unwise, foolish, reckless decision to pass up that opportunity to get gas.

See, he told himself, he had even had time to conjure up a bunch of words to describe his dumb decision to not stop at that gas station.

Heck, he could have even gotten a snack and something to drink and then he wouldn't be in this situation now. What a mess. He could have been home hours ago.

He decided not to wait. He could be here all night and who knows how long it would be in the morning until someone came along.

He got out of the car and locked the doors. He decided he would start walking until he got beyond the trees so he could call his dad. His parents might be wondering what happened to him. No, he knew they wouldn't miss him until in the morning. They went to bed by ten o'clock because they both went to work early and they very rarely stayed up late.

Maybe he could call his grandfather. He might be closer. Logan figured that he was about halfway, so either one would work ... his dad or his grandfather. His grandfather would be up early anyway to tend to the animals on the farm.

He started to walk. He hadn't realized how windy it was. The cold wind bit sharply at his nose and cheeks. All he had was a windbreaker to shield him from the weather.

When he left home he figured he'd be in the car the whole time so what would be the purpose of wearing some heavy coat that would make him too hot. Besides, it wasn't stormy when he left for the farm in the early morning. He hadn't paid any attention to the weather forecast on the radio.

He started to wonder if this decision to walk was as stupid and ill-advised as his failure to stop at the service station. He was getting colder. His sneakers and thin socks weren't holding up very well against the weather out here. His feet were wet from stepping in the puddles along the side of the road.

He looked up at the road ahead of him. The fog was clinging to the trees on either side of the road. They looked like they were wrapped in spider webs and that was a little unnerving. He had never liked spiders. He would come across spiders, big spiders, in his grandfather's barn and they always gave him the creeps.

When the wind blew, ragged strips of fog drifted across the road like big sheets of cobwebs. He didn't like cobwebs either. The outbuildings on the farm always had cobwebs. The sight gave him a chill.

This was probably the scariest situation he had ever been in. He decided that he would be making better choices in the future. This was a real wake-up call for him. His parents had talked to him about things like wise choices and stuff like that, but he thought he knew what he was doing. "Yeah, yeah, okay," had been his response to them. Now he saw that their advice should have been taken to heart.

He had walked about a mile down the road when he stopped suddenly. Wait! He heard something – it was over in the trees beside the road! Then he heard something moving along through the underbrush. He realized he was suddenly scared.

He didn't know what it was, but it didn't sound good. He kept walking. He realized that he was walking slowly and cautiously like he was creeping along so as not to be heard. He knew that he wasn't sneaking by because, whatever it was out in the woods already knew that he was there. He started to walk a little faster. He thought that, if he hurried, he might be able to get farther away from whatever it was. He would *love* to get past whatever it was – especially before he had to see it. Seeing it might send him right over the edge.

Was it a cougar, or maybe a bear? He knew that black bears follow you along for a while before they attacked you. Was if a wolf? Oh, no, he knew he shouldn't have thought of that one.

He had seen the movie where the two boys traveling across country were told by the villagers to stay on the road. They were also walking in the fog and, when they got off the road, they were attacked by werewolves. Then, in his imagination, Logan could picture a werewolf lurking in the trees, stalking him, and waiting to jump on him.

He suddenly heard a cry and a squeal. Okay! Okay! He knew that something was definitely out there now! He was afraid that he could be the next victim of the squealing, snarling, biting monster that was tracking him along the road. He realized that he might not get far enough to make that phone call to his parents. And, if he was lucky enough to even make the call, would he still be alive when someone got there to rescue him?

103

Wait! He heard the monster again, sneaking along through the trees. The snapping twigs gave it away. It sounded like it was close, *really* close.

He had never been a screamer, but he realized that he might be making an exception here – real soon. Then, he heard sounds on the other side of the road. He moved to the center of the road and started walking faster.

Now, there was more than one monster. Maybe it was a whole family of werewolves looking to feast on someone. He was the only victim to have come along the deserted road tonight. So, he was it! He would be dinner for a whole pack of werewolves.

He never imagined that something like this could ever happen to him, but he, for sure, could imagine it now ... his throat torn out, his arms and legs gnawed off, and his heart ripped out. He could imagine the monsters fighting over which one got to eat it while it was still warm and beating. Ugh! The thought made him feel sick and he was terrified.

His active imagination was on overload now – it was running some really crazy thoughts through his head, and he was scaring himself to death. He realized that there were tears in his eyes and he knew that he had never, ever been this scared in his whole life. He was panicked beyond rational thought.

Maybe he should send a good-bye text to his parents and thank them for their good advice; that great advice that he had not followed. He looked down at his phone. There was still no service. He wouldn't even be able to let anybody know what happened to him and they would probably never even find his body. The werewolves would pick apart his skeleton and gnaw on his bones once they had eaten all the good stuff.

He would disappear forever and everyone would always wonder what happened to him, but no one would ever know. He would just vanish ... he'd be gone ... eaten in the woods and what was left of his bones scattered all over the place!

He had a funny thought. The football team at school would have to get a new wide receiver. He smiled slightly at the thought, but the humor did nothing to relieve him of his terrified feeling.

He started to run. Maybe he could outrun them. That never seemed to happen in the movies, but he knew he that was a pretty fast runner. He might reach a house somewhere up ahead before they could attack him.

As he ran he could feel the tears from his eyes being blown back toward his ears as they came out of his eyes. He was very aware of just how dire the situation was.

He had heard that thousands of people disappear without a trace every year and they are never found. His friend, Todd, had joked that aliens were picking them up using them for food. It was funny at the time but now that possibility didn't seem so farfetched. Between the aliens, the werewolves, and the bears, he didn't think he would stand a chance.

Wait! He heard a sound in the distance behind him. He turned to look back over his shoulder. He saw two pinpoints of light coming toward him down the road through the thick fog. Oh, no, they were attacking! This was the moment! He could see the bright eyes of the werewolf racing down the road, trying to catch up to him.

He was petrified. He was almost too scared to move! He didn't think he couldn't run any farther. It wouldn't do him any good to run anyway. The werewolf was probably so much faster than he was. What should he do now?

He moved to the side of the road and squatted down. He covered his eyes with his fists and waited for what he knew was about to happen. He held his breath in expectation of what was his inevitable fate.

All of this was happening, he thought, because he was too irresponsible to stop for a few minutes and get gas when he knew the gas tank was low. He was so stupid. He was so sorry, but now it was too late. He could hear the sounds coming closer, like a low growling. He was convinced that it must be what werewolves sounded like before they attacked. He hunched down and waited.

Wait! Suddenly, a vehicle stopped in the road in front of him! No attack? He uncovered his eyes and looked up. There was an old pickup truck in the road.

There was an older man in the driver's seat. He leaned over and rolled down the passenger window. "You having a problem there, Sonny?" he asked.

Logan jumped up and ran over to the truck. He jerked open the passenger door and jumped into the vehicle. He was breathing heavy. He slammed the door, rolled up the window, and then he locked the door.

"Drive, drive!" he shouted.

"Whoa, there, Sonny," the driver said. "What's seems to be the problem here?"

"There's a werewolf after me!" Logan shouted breathlessly. "He's gonna get me. He's been chasing me all along the road."

"Well, Sonny, there ain't no werewolves in these parts around here. They live on the other side of the mountains," the old man said, and he chuckled.

"You don't understand," Logan said. "I'm sure a werewolf was following me."

"No, Sonny," the man answered, "there ain't no werewolves 'round here, regular wolves neither. I should know. I've been living here forever."

"No? Well, then it's a bear," Logan said. "It's been stalking me for a long way. I've been hearing it in the trees all the way along."

"Now, Sonny," said the old man, "those bears live farther up the mountains. They don't come down this far. There ain't no bears and no werewolves either. You're spooked, that's all – letting your imagination run away with you."

The old man kept talking. "I saw your car on the side of the road back a ways and I was looking out for you. I almost missed you, all hunkered down in the dark over there. It's just a really bad night to be out. But, there ain't nothing out there that's gonna hurt you in any way."

"But, I heard it," Logan said.

The old man smiled at him.

"No, really," Logan added, "on both sides of the road. It was monsters. They were following all along and they were getting ready to jump me when you came along. You saved my life."

Then the old man chuckled again. "Whoa, there, Sonny," he said. "Reel back in that imagination of yours. You're just spooked 'cause it's dark and gloomy out there. That could get to anyone out on a night like this. The sounds you heard are most likely just deer and elk foraging in the forest. They're out at night looking for something to eat. They can make all kinds of racket out there, what with those antlers dragging through the bushes and grasses beneath them trees out there. There's nothing else out there. Those animals won't hurt you none."

"Are you sure?" Logan asked. "I thought I heard growling and stuff."

"No, Sonny," the man answered. "Those elk make all kinds of sounds to warn off the others trying to horn in on their territory where they're eating. That's all you heard."

"But I heard squealing and stuff," Logan added.

"Sonny, that's just the owls catching rabbits. The rabbits tend to do some crying and squealing when they're caught. There ain't nothing to be afraid of out here. I've lived 'round here for nigh on 82 years and I ain't never been attacked by no werewolves and no bears. It ain't gonna happen. So, where you headed."

"My car ran out of gas and my cell phone didn't have any service," Logan explained. "I waited a couple of hours and I decided to walk."

"Well, you're all right now." The old man assured him. "It might have been wiser for you to wait in the car on a night like this. It's some rough weather we've been having this week, but you're okay now. I got a can of gas in the back of the truck. I'll take you back to your car and get you on your way."

"Thank you," Logan said, and he was very relieved, and very sincere. "Thank you so much."

Logan took a deep breath and settled back in the seat. He had to smile at how foolish he had been. He had let his imagination get the best of him. He was glad that none of the guys on the football team would ever find about how scared he had been ... even crying and thinking about screaming. That was really dumb. The guys would never stop teasing him. In the future, he decided, he would definitely make better choices.

The End

Millie

Millie was a very sharp-eyed twelve-year-old. She considered herself to be really smart because she always paid close attention to everything around her. She was good at solving puzzles and mazes and she liked to figure out riddles.

A big storm came up in the late afternoon. The heavy clouds rolled in and it got dark early. The storm didn't bother her. She was not afraid of storms. She thought the lightning was cool. She loved the way the streaks of lightning raced across the sky in strange patterns. It was fun to watch.

The thunder was a little different. It was noisy. She didn't really care for loud sounds, but if she had to put up with the thunder to see the lightning, then it was okay with her.

The rain dripping off the leaves of the tree outside her window made the tree look sad. She had written a story about the sad tree and turned it in for a project in her English class.

Now, she was working on a project for her History class. She had to create a booklet about indigenous peoples who lived in Washington State and write about the differences between the coastal peoples and the people who lived on the plateau. She had already written down the information she wanted to put in the booklet.

Millie had put together the blank pages, folded them in half, and stapled them together in the middle to make a booklet. It looked perfect. Next, she had written the information inside about how the tribes were similar and how they were different in their religion, their trading habits, and their cultures.

The only thing left to do was to draw pictures in the booklet that her teacher called *illustrations* and to color them. She had spent more than an hour carefully sketching out her pictures and then going over the lines with ink, once she was satisfied that she wouldn't have to erase any more.

She was sitting on her bed. She was busy arranging her colored pencils, and getting ready to color her pictures. She wanted to be sure to do a good a job to bring her pictures to life. She felt that it would really make her booklet special.

Wait! Suddenly a mouse ran out from under her bed and raced out the door into the hallway! Millie froze in place.

"Oh!" a little sound escaped from her mouth. She didn't mean for that to happen. It was just so sudden that it surprised her.

She didn't like mice. Once, when she was in the garage, the wind blew the door closed and before she could get out, she saw two mice running across the floor. It was kind of dark in the garage and they scared her. Ever since then she hoped that she would never see another mouse.

Millie watched the doorway. A minute or two later the mouse ran back into her room and disappeared under her bed. She didn't panic. She wasn't that kind of person. After all, she told herself, she was safe on her bed. And ... she wasn't about to scream out for her mother. She liked to solve her problems on her own. Unless it was an emergency, she would *not* be yelling for help.

She waited for the sound of a mouse but she didn't hear any kind of squeaking. As she sat there, the mouse abruptly ran out from under the bed and into the hall again!

Wait! She thought that something was weird about the mouse. She wasn't quite sure what it was, but something about the mouse was out of place. She just couldn't put her finger on it, but she knew something wasn't right. But, it had run across the room too quickly for her to really get a good look.

She took a breath, she put down her pencils, and she waited. She watched the doorway closely. She was determined to get a good look at that mouse! In just a couple of minutes, the mouse ran back from the hallway to disappear under her bed.

But, this time, she *did* get a good look at it. She was proud of her ability to pay attention. What she saw was ... the feet of the mouse weren't moving. That was really curious.

Millie thought about that – a mouse that runs without moving its feet. Now, that *was* weird. She wondered what it meant. She turned her attention to figuring it out. Ah ... in just a couple of minutes she felt that she had the answer.

She watched for the mouse again. She wanted to see if her idea was correct. When the mouse ran out from under her bed and into the hall again, she knew she was right. The mouse was a fake!

Now, how does a mouse, that's not real, run across the room? That was the next problem for her to solve. She watched for the mouse to return. When it did, Millie looked closely and she saw light reflecting off a string that was attached behind it. That was it! The mouse wasn't real, and it had a string attached to it.

Then she knew what was going on – someone must be trying to scare her. Millie knew that the only ones who would do that were her two brothers, Tyler and Gordon. She had figured it out! She smiled. Once again her ability to pay attention had helped her solve a problem.

This wasn't the first time her brothers had tried to scare her. They had tried a number of times in the past. After their tricks worked the first few times, she had figured them out every time and their tricks failed. She had spoiled their fun many times.

Millie decided that, because the storm was making everything dark and scary, they thought they would try to frighten her with their trick. They were pulling the mouse out into the hall from under the bed, and then pulling it back again. They were pulling the mouse back and forth with the string.

That meant only one thing – one of them was under her bed and the other one was out in the hall. Even though their scary tricks didn't work, they kept trying. She smiled at the thought they would keep at it, even though they failed time after time. That's why she never panicked when she saw something weird.

She knew just what to do. She stretched out across the bed, leaned over the side, and looked under the bed.

"Hey, Tyler," she said, "whatcha doing down there?"

Her brother jumped in surprise and bumped his head. "Ouch!" he said, "are you trying to give me a heart attack?"

She answered, "Are you trying to give me one? It looks like you and Gordon are trying to pull a fast one here."

"Uh, what are you talking about?" Tyler asked.

"I just caught you red-handed," Millie said. "You can't deny what you two are doing. Don't try to play innocent. If you're not doing anything, then explain why you are lying on the floor under my bed. That's not a normal place for you to be, so you just tell me how you came to be under there."

At that moment Gordon came into the room. "Darn!" he said. "Our trick didn't work, again!"

"That's right," Millie said.

Tyler rolled out from under the bed and asked, "How did you figure it out?"

"It was so easy," Millie answered. "You two didn't fool me for a minute. The feet on that mouse weren't moving and I saw the light reflecting off the string you have tied to it. Simple."

The boys started out of the room. Millie could see that they were disappointed.

"Next time," Gordon said, looking back over his shoulder. "One of these times we're going to get you."

"I'm looking forward to it," Millie said. She liked the challenge. She picked up her colored pencils again and opened her booklet.

The End

It was a dark and stormy night ...

Nancy

Nancy was ill – and she *hated* being ill. She had been 'under the weather' for five days, as her grandmother called it. That was five long days of misery ... with the coughing and the runny nose and the headaches. It was five days of not going to school and five days of not seeing her friends. She was just miserable.

Plus, both of her parents had to go out of town on business. Her parents owned their own business and that required her father to go out of town sometimes on trips. But, this new trip was a little different. There were two business meetings scheduled, in two different cities, and even though they tried, they were not able to change the days. They explained that there were just too many factors involved and too many other people would be affected, so the appointments couldn't be changed. They *had* to go. They decided that Nancy's mother would go to one meeting and her father would attend the other one.

They didn't want to leave Nancy because she was ill, but her grandmother stepped in and took Nancy to *her* house. She promised Nancy's parents that she would cure their 'little girl' before they returned, using her old-fashioned remedies.

So, off to her grandparents' house she went. Any other time she would have been delighted to go to their house. But, being sick, she wasn't in the mood for much of anything. She didn't want to do anything except sleep. She was tired all the time and she just ached all over. It was the flu and she didn't like it. She hadn't been sick in two years.

Nancy had been at her grandparents' house for three days. Her grandmother put her on the sofa in the living room. She said she wanted to keep an eye on her and she wasn't able to run up and down the stairs all day to look after her.

So, Nancy was bundled up on the sofa with orange juice, a hot water bottle, and a tissue box on the coffee table in front of her.

There had been three long days of hot water bottles and smelly liniment on her chest, medicated steam from the machine on the coffee table, and chicken soup.

There had also been three days of some weird potions that her grandmother cooked up from herbs and spices. She said that *her* grandmother made it for her when she was sick as a child. Wow, Nancy thought to herself, it was bitter and it tasted like maybe her great, great grandmother had made *this* batch too. Nancy called the ingredients twigs and leaves – but she only said that to herself.

There were also a couple of books on the coffee table that she had brought with her from home. They were Nancy Drew mystery books. Nancy Drew was her favorite character that she had ever found in books. She thought Nancy Drew was smart and so clever.

Her mother told her that she *also* loved the Nancy Drew books when she was growing up, so she named her daughter after her favorite character. That's how Nancy got her name. She was very proud of being named after such an awesome character.

Nancy would read the books and get very involved in the story, trying to solve each mystery before it was revealed in the book. She pretended that *she* was the Nancy in the book and she followed every clue from every case.

Her mother said that she had a very 'vivid' imagination. Nancy learned that it meant she had a good imagination and it helped her enjoy every story by opening up a secret world for her in the books she read. She could picture everything that she was reading in her head. The images she created in her mind were very clear. She loved *that* part of reading. Reading was her favorite pastime.

She hadn't felt well enough the past few days to read, but she really wanted to get into the books she had on the table. She kept looking at them, but they just sat there silently.

"So, I guess you aren't going to read yourselves to me," she said to them. They didn't answer. They just sat there waiting for her to make the next move – which would be to pick them up and open them.

Then, during the night, a big thunder storm swooped into the area. The lightning and thunder woke her up and kept her from getting back to sleep. The rain against the window was annoying to her. Well, almost everything annoyed her since she didn't feel well, but she tried not to let it show. She smiled and tried to be hopeful with her grandmother's potions.

The first couple of days had been the worse. She felt like she had never been sicker than she was this time. Of course, since she hadn't been sick for so long, she had trouble remembering how she felt back at the time. She wasn't sure she could compare and be fair about it. She described herself as a fair and practical person. All of her friends agreed that she was correct in her evaluation of herself.

Sometime the day before, Nancy started feeling better. She wondered if it was her grandmother's 'cures' that were doing the trick, but she couldn't be certain. She considered that maybe the flu was just tired of being there and was simply passing on.

Well, she thought, since the annoying storm came to bother her, and it didn't appear as if it was in any hurry to move on, and since she couldn't get back to sleep, she decided it was the perfect time to read.

She had been reading for an hour or so, when her grandmother came into the room. She said that breakfast would be along in a few minutes. She said her grandfather was out running errands. She added that he would stop by the store for more orange juice, but in the meantime, she had some prune juice that would be perfect for breakfast.

Yuck! Nancy decided she was *not* looking forward to breakfast. When her grandmother brought in the breakfast tray a little later, Nancy decided that she *really* wasn't looking forward to *this* breakfast! Sure enough, there was a glass of dark, purple juice on the tray. But, what made her grimace was the big bowl sitting next to the juice. She wasn't exactly sure what it was, but it didn't look like *anything* she had ever seen before.

She poked at the bowl of breakfast with a spoon. When she hesitated, her grandmother assured that it was a wonderful dish that would be very good for her stomach and that it would have her up and around in no time. Nancy wasn't so sure. She looked at the strange mixture ... another of her grandmother's potions, she decided. It was a big bowl of milk with a piece of toast pressed into it and on the top was a poached egg!

So, she said to herself, it wasn't bad enough that she had to be sick, but she had to be tortured with weird food too. She went ahead and ate a few bites of the breakfast. It wasn't too bad – not as bad as she thought it would be. It tasted much better than it looked in the bowl.

She wasn't so sure her stomach would welcome this home remedy that her grandmother was so sure was good for it. She waited for the breakfast to come back up, but it didn't.

She was so looking forward to getting over the flu so she could have some real food. She knew that her stomach would much prefer a big bowl of macaroni and cheese and probably some cookies and potato chips ... maybe a little ice cream to top it off.

After she had eaten some of the food and drank some of the weird-tasting juice, her grandmother took away the tray. Nancy wished that she had some candy, or some gum, or *something* to help get rid of the taste of the juice. She made a mental note that she would never *voluntarily* drink prune juice again.

Nancy decided to forget that she had actually eaten some of that breakfast concoction. She put the whole experience behind her and looked forward to lunch, which would probably be chicken soup. She knew that at least it wouldn't leave a bitter taste in her mouth.

She picked up her book from the table and started reading from where she left off. After a while she fell asleep with the book on her chest.

Some kind of sound woke her up. It wasn't loud. It was kind of muffled and she couldn't place it, but it was enough to get her attention and make her open her eyes. She wasn't sure how long she had been asleep. She didn't think it was long enough for her to fall into a deep sleep. She figured that she just drifted off and she was pretty sure it hadn't been *that* long.

She looked at the ceiling for a moment. She felt like something was different. She couldn't put her finger on it, but the feeling was there. She pushed her Nancy Drew skills forward in her mind and she listened. The house was quiet. That was a little unnerving. There were usually sounds all the time from somewhere in the house, but now it seemed eerily silent.

She wondered if maybe her grandmother was taking her nap. But, when she was napping, her grandfather would be puttering around. He always had a list of things to do – something to keep him busy and active, he liked to say.

Nancy half sat up and looked around. The book that was open on her chest slid down to her lap. She looked around and she started to lie back down when something caught her attention.

She was proud of her Nancy Drew observation skills. She had learned from her reading to pay attention and to notice everything around her. Her eyes went directly to a pair of boots that were sitting under the window, below the drapes. She was certain they hadn't been there before.

She wondered where they came from. And ... she wondered why boots would be there anyway. It seemed like such an odd place for them to be. She looked at them for a few minutes. She was *very* positive they weren't there earlier. After all, she had been in that room for three days and she had seen everything in the room there was to see – and those boots had definitely not been there before.

Wait! The drapes above the boots suddenly moved a little! Nancy thought she could feel her heart stop. She felt a chill racing through her body! What did it mean? Why were the boots sitting there and why were the drapes moving?

Her brain was trying to make a connection. An idea started forming in her head and, as it took shape, she became even more afraid. All at once the idea became crystal clear – someone was standing behind the drapes!

She heard her own sharp intake of breath and she clamped her hand over her mouth to muffle the sound. Someone was standing behind the drapes and she didn't want to be heard. If she made a sound, whoever was there would know that she was awake!

Even though she was scared to death, and afraid to move, she knew she had to do something. She groped around inside herself for her Nancy Drew skills and she pushed them into the front of her mind. If Nancy Drew were here, what would she do? That thought made her feel braver, and more confident. She felt more in control and less afraid. After all, she told herself, she was a very practical person. She should be able to figure this out.

Nancy tried to sort out her options. She knew that she dare not scream. Should she investigate? Should she just go over there and yank back the drapes to reveal the person hiding back there? No ... that was foolish. She shouldn't confront the person, not by herself. Should she run – would she get very far if she did? She looked around the room. Wait! The drapes shifted and moved again! She was nervous and she felt very cold. She thought, maybe she should quietly get up and sneak out of the room.

Then she wondered something else – where were her grandparents? Why was the house so quiet? Had something happened to them? She was worried. She had another thought in her practical mind ... if something *did* happen to them, then why would someone feel the need to hide behind the drapes?

She decided that her very best option was to sneak out of the room and go for help. She believed that, if she were really quiet, she would have a good head start if the person behind the drapes realized that she was leaving the room. She was thinking that the best plan would be to go out the front door and run to a neighbor's house.

She was determined to put her plan into action but her whole body felt heavy, like it wasn't able to move. She thought that maybe being afraid caused your body to get sluggish. No way, she said to herself, this can't happen. She scolded herself for being so scared that she couldn't move. After all, she said to herself, she was in control, right?

She slowly, and very softly, took the book from her lap and put it on the floor. Holding her breath, she quietly slid her feet and legs out from under the blankets. She stopped to listen.

She took a few deep breaths and let the air out slowly to help her calm down and she braced herself. She could feel her heart beating against her chest and she felt a little shaky. She worried that her legs might not hold her up.

She took a look over toward the drapes. They were still moving, but the boots had not shifted. They were still in the same place. She was sure that she had not been heard. As she was positioning herself to slip out from under the covers and creep toward the door, her grandmother suddenly came into the room.

She said, "My gracious, child, whatever are you up to in here?"

"Grandma," Nancy whispered, "someone's over there behind those drapes!" She pointed.

"There's no one there, child," her grandmother answered.

Nancy didn't say anything. She just pointed at the boots on the floor below the drapes.

Her grandmother's face broke into a huge smile and she chuckled. "Well, Miss Nancy Drew, there is no mystery here," she said. "You've been reading too many of those books."

Nancy was confused by her reaction.

Her grandmother marched over to the drapes and flung them back to reveal the window behind them. Nancy looked down and saw that the boots were empty. They were just sitting there.

"But, the drapes were moving," she said, but her grandmother shook her head.

"Child," she said, "you certainly do have one heck of an imagination. Those are just your grandpa's boots. After his errands, his boots were wet, so he put them here by the heating vent to dry. He does that all the time. The heat coming up from the vent was moving those drapes around. It was nothing more than that. There's no big mystery here."

Nancy felt so relieved.

"You get yourself back under those blankets," her grandmother directed. "The only mysteries around here will be in those books you have there. Land sakes, you are as bad as your mother, seeing mysteries everywhere you go."

The End

It was a dark and stormy night ...

Olivia

"Olivia Charlotte Madeline Greenway does not like storms," Charlie said aloud, as she wrote the words in her diary. "And especially the thunder part of it!" she added. She took extra care to make sure she included that exclamation point. To her, it was very important to add that at the end of every sentence she felt her diary should pay attention to. Sometimes she added two exclamation points.

She had received the diary for her birthday from one of her grandmothers and she immediately saw it as a sign. She felt that it was an important sign, an omen, that she should carefully detail *every single thing* in her life that had special meaning.

She wanted to be sure that her own private diary, the book that held the all of the most valuable details of her life story was as accurate as possible. It could be very important to her at some point – particularly to remind her of all these vital facts.

She had listed all the many things that she wasn't very fond of – like spiders, and snakes, and bees, and mud puddles, and goats. Well, she had never actually even met a goat, but she was *sure* she wouldn't like them. After all, they ate flowers and flowers were one of the things that she liked the most. All the things that she liked were wisely listed in a separate section.

The very first thing on her list of the things she wasn't fond of was her name. She was named after the mothers of her grandmothers, or some ancient ancestors or something. Charlie never could quite get that story straight.

But, she didn't care, not one bit, how many of her great grandmothers she was named after. She felt her parents should have made a different choice. They told her they had trouble narrowing down the names, and they didn't want anyone to feel slighted, so they just added them all in. She was doomed to suffer forever with her name. She had added three exclamation points after that entry! Her poor, older sister had to suffer with the names of the current grandmothers, and that was just as bad, if you asked Charlie. She added three exclamation points to that entry in her diary too!

Her mother called her Olivia Charlotte. She was absolutely *not* fond of that. She had never understood why her mother couldn't just use one of the names on her list of 'given names' as her mother called them. Charlie would have been happier if they had given them to someone else. One name would have been plenty. After all, there wasn't anyone else, not for a hundred miles, who was going to answer to any of those names anyway.

Her father called her his sugar doughnut. That went onto the page of the things she liked.

Her grandmother on her father's side called her Madeline. Geez ... and that was painful to hear. Her father's dad called her Tuffy because she was a bit of a tomboy. That also went onto the page of things she especially liked.

Her grandmother on her mother's side called her Charlotte. That wasn't too bad. At least it wasn't as painful to hear, but it still sounded *way* old. Her mother's dad called her Squeaky. He said that she sounded like a little mouse when she cried as a baby. Huh! Mice had been promptly added to her dislike page, so she couldn't relate to that name either.

Since everyone called her something different, it was difficult to know how to answer each person. But, she knew they were talking to her because there wasn't anyone that she knew of who had all of her names, so it was very obvious that they were talking to her.

To her friends, she was Charlie, just plain old Charlie. Now, *that* was her favorite. That also had three exclamation points in her book. When anyone at school called her one of the names from her dislike list, she immediately corrected them. She had insisted so often, that even her teachers called her Charlie.

While she was writing, thunder boomed outside her window, which made her jump. She looked at the entry in the diary about the thunder. She thought about it for a moment or two and then she added another exclamation point.

She had always been afraid of thunder storms. The wind, the rain, the thunder, and the lightning had scared her for as far back as she could remember. Most of her life she had immediately gone to her sister's room whenever a storm showed up.

Becca always expected Charlie and she let her snuggle under her covers during storms. Rebecca Estelle Gwendolyn Greenway; that was her name – and *that* was a little hard for Charlie to write in her diary. She wasn't sure that she would leave it in there either. It was a little embarrassing and she was glad Becca wouldn't ever know that she wrote it down.

Just like Charlie, Becca never liked *her* name either. Charlie didn't blame her ... no way ... not one teeny, tiny bit. But, because she was named after the current grandmothers, Becca pretended to be proud of her name, especially when they were around. But, Charlie knew better. But, her sister was Becca to her, and she was Becca to her friends, the ones who went off to college with her a couple of weeks ago.

Charlie tried really hard not to feel abandoned when Becca left for school with her friends. She knew it was important and besides, she promised to come home for holidays and school breaks.

With Becca gone, the house seemed like a big, old barn. It was a really gigantic two story house, complete with a full basement and attic. To Charlie that counted as four stories.

But, her parents always called it their big, two-story dream house. Go figure, Charlie said to herself. Her parents called themselves 'unconventional' or something like that. They bought the house when they first got married. They had spent all these umpteen years fixing it up, and remodeling it, and repairing the big old house they had named *Greenway Place*.

Charlie used to add an extra 'a' to make it 'palace' and she told everyone she lived in a palace. When her grandmothers and her mother's friends would coo her, and pinch her cheeks, and call her a princess, she stopped doing that.

After all, she wasn't sure how many princesses climbed trees, and played baseball with the boys, and arm wrestled the boys, but she didn't believe there could be very many.

Well, her parents were very happy with their big, old dream house, so Charlie couldn't really blame them for their choice. If they really wanted to live in this drafty, old house, then she had no problem going along with them and pretending to love it too. She was quite happy here.

Someday, when she was older, she intended to live in a small brick house somewhere that wasn't on a hill like Greenway Place.

Since Becca left, Charlie knew she would have to suffer alone during thunder storms. A storm, a week ago, had been especially scary. A big limb from the huge tree outside her room broke off and fell against the house. There was some damage. A window was broken and the wall was damaged. Her father called it cosmetic. She wasn't exactly sure what that meant.

But there were some cracks made along the edge of the house. It was weird because the ceiling in her room looked like it was pushed a little bit away from the wall where the tree limb hit the house. Her father told her not to worry about it, that the ceiling wouldn't fall down. He said he would just add it to his *fix-it list*. He was repairing the damage as time permitted. He promised to seal up everything after he finished replacing the window up there in the attic.

That was just fine with Charlie. The damage didn't have any effect on her room where all her treasures were carefully displayed or properly stored so as to preserve them forever and ever.

She could hear the wind outside, blowing the rain against the window. The raindrops, which Charlie figured should be soft, because they were just water, sounded like little stones hitting against the window. Wow, she thought, the wind must be blowing much harder than when she got home from school.

Then she thought about Becca. She left early for college because she said she wanted to take some summer classes. She wanted to jump right into college and not wait until the end of summer to start.

Charlie's school would be over in two weeks and she had great plans for the summer. Becca said she could come and visit her at college for a week. She was looking forward to that.

She had also promised George, the boy down the street, that she would help him build a treehouse in the big oak tree in his backyard. She had also promised Eddie, another boy in the neighborhood, that she would help him build a new pen for his rabbits.

She listened to the rain pinging against the windows for a few minutes. She was lost in thought and so she forgot to brace herself for the thunder.

When the lightning flashed right outside the window and the thunder boomed loudly, she almost jumped out of bed. Oh-h-h … she should have been ready for that. She really didn't like to be surprised. She went back to her diary and added another exclamation point to the note about the thunder.

Charlie was getting a little scared. The storm sounded like it might be getting closer and getting worse. She wondered if she would feel any better if she went and slept in Becca's room. Nah … without Becca there with her, it would be cold and lonely.

Besides, she already had this conversation with herself. She was thirteen now, that was practically almost an adult. She had vowed that, if she had any bravery, she would find it and she would push it to the front of her mind and not ever be afraid again. After all, she wasn't about to be someone's scared little princess who lived in that palace on the hill. She knew that she was so much tougher than that.

There had been many storms over the years and not a one of them had ever hurt her, she reasoned. So, then, what was there to be afraid of? It made good sense, but it still scared her.

She figured she would have to practice being brave for a while before it could take effect and not bother her so much. But, she would tough it out.

She wasn't about to go to her parents room for protection. She hadn't gone to their room scared of a storm since she was something like three years old!

Well, Becca had always been there, so there wasn't any reason to go all the way down to the far end of the hall to her parents' room when Becca's room was right directly across the hall from hers. So, she just went to Becca and everything had always worked out perfectly.

While she was thinking all of that through, the lamp beside her bed blinked. Oh, boy, she thought, I hope the power doesn't go out. Pitch dark in a storm? No, way! That would really test her new bravery and she definitely had not practiced long enough for it to withstand a storm *and* a power outage!

Should she get up and find her candles, she wondered? She knew that she kept some candles somewhere in one of her dresser drawers because the power had gone out before. No, she didn't want to get up. She was a little too afraid.

The lamp wasn't very strong and outside the small circle of its light, the room was shadowy and gloomy. The room was kind of spooky, now that she thought about it, as she looked around the room.

Something caught her attention across the room. There was something on the wall, up near the ceiling, where there was that little split between the ceiling and the wall. She leaned forward and strained her eyes to peer into the eerie darkness on the far side of the room.

What was that, she asked herself? She couldn't make it out. There shouldn't be anything up there. It wasn't a bug or anything like that. That would be one spot, not the bunch that she could see moving down the wall.

Was it ants, like columns of ants moving down from the ceiling toward her dresser? No, maybe not. She could remember her father telling her that ants didn't wander around this high up because they could find what they were looking for on the ground outside or maybe in the basement. There wasn't any good reason for them to use up all their energy climbing all the way up here.

He said that if the ants found something way up here, they would have to haul it all the way back down to the ground. He promised her that ants were way too practical and sensible to go to all that trouble.

That thought didn't seem to comfort her very much, when something was crawling down from the attic, down through that crack along the wall. Something was invading her room in a thunder storm, something that wasn't supposed to be there! It wasn't something that was as sensible as the ants!

She was getting more scared. Brave or not, she could see something that should *not* be there! As she tried to understand what was happening, she slowly reached out her hand and turned up the lamp so she could see across the room.

As the room got brighter, she could see streaks of red running down the wall from the ceiling. It must have been at least ten streaks of red running slowly down the wall.

Wait! It was blood! She stared at the wall. It was BLOOD! She was seeing blood running down her walls!

Suddenly, Charlie couldn't find her bravery. She swallowed hard and she tried again, but there was absolutely no bravery anywhere inside of her. Tomboy or not, Tuffy or not, she was instantly a girl – somebody's little princess living in that palace on the hill. She screamed bloody murder at the very tip-top of her lungs.

When she ran out of breath, she took a *really* deep breath to fill her lungs with air, and she sent out her second blood curdling scream. She held that scream for as long as her breath could keep it going!

Suddenly, her mother burst into the room. She stopped in the doorway.

"Olivia Charlotte!" she yelled in panic. "What is it?" What's happened?"

Charlie was terrified! She was out of breath and her eyes were open just as far as she could open them. She looked like she was frozen in place. She tried to catch her breath, but she was finding it difficult. She tried to talk, to explain to her mother what was happening, but no words came out. All she could do was to point to the bloody streaks on the wall across from her.

Her mother turned and looked at the wall where Charlie pointed. She looked back at Charlie's wild, wide-eyed, expression. Then, she looked back to the wall, and then back to Charlie again.

She flipped on the overhead light. She put her hands on her hips and turned toward the door. "James!" she yelled back over her shoulder. "James!"

"What is it?" Charlie's father called from the far end of the hall.

"You left the attic door open! The dog must have been up there and she spilled the sealer and the paint you were using in the attic. It's running down the wall in here!"

Charlie could hear her father coming down the hall from their bedroom. He stopped in the doorway and he stood looking at the wall. "Interesting," was all he said and he shook his head, almost as if he thought it looked really cool.

Her mother came over and sat on the edge of the bed. She put her arms around Charlie. "It's only paint," she said. "Your father will clean it up. Don't you worry – we'll add that to our *fix-it* list and get your room re-painted."

Charlie wasn't sure if she felt comforted or not. Her throat hurt. After all, tomboys weren't known for screaming, so her throat wasn't used to that.

"You can pick out any color you want," her mother added. "You can even have wall paper if you think you'd like that better."

Charlie just nodded her head and leaned against her mother's shoulder. It was going to take her a few minutes to recover from that scare – and that scream. She hoped her parents wouldn't tell anyone about her screaming. She decided that she would definitely *not* write anything about this in her diary.

The End

It was a dark and stormy night ...

Puddles

Puddles loved the rain. She loved stormy days. Thunder and lightning didn't bother her one bit. On rainy days she could sit at her window for hours watching the dark clouds rolling across the sky. She loved the fresh smell of the rain and everything seemed so clean and bright and new after it rained.

In the evenings she would sit by the window and do her homework. When it rained, her mother would insist that she keep the window closed because she didn't want the rain water to pool up in the window sill or soak the carpet in front of the window. That poor old carpet had gotten soaked a number of times.

Puddles dutifully kept the window closed during the rain. She was a little disappointed at the idea, but she could understand her mother's concern. But, when it rained, Puddles would be right there, even with the window shut, looking through the glass and watching those storm clouds gathering and sweeping across the sky. They were so magnificent.

Her mother told her that, when she was little, she would run to every mud puddle and splash through it. She told her that she always wanted to go outside when it rained. She would be walking along when, suddenly, she would throw her little umbrella up into the air and race for the nearest mud puddle.

That's how she got her nickname. Her given name was Annamaria, which took too much time to say, in her opinion. So, everyone picked up on the nickname her mother had given her and they all called her Puddles. Even though she was now a seventh grader, all of her friends still called her Puddles.

It had been raining all day. After school she had volleyball practice. When she got home from school she finished her chores, and after eating dinner with her family, she was *finally* able to escape to her room. There were clouds outside that needed watching. The idea that they would go racing by without her seeing them was a little upsetting.

Earlier, there had been some lightning and some thunder, but they had already passed over. Now, there was a little wind, but plenty of clouds. Puddles finished her homework, after stopping several times to stare out the window at the clouds.

The moon was very bright, but when the clouds covered it, everything outside was very dark. She decided that she liked the idea of the contrast. The light and then dark and then light again, seemed really dramatic to her. She liked the notion that Mother Nature was so creative.

While she was looking out the window at the backyard, the clouds swept away from the moon and the yard was bathed in bright light. She caught her breath suddenly when she looked at the fence running across the rear of the yard. There was a shadow on the fence! She watched it because it seemed to move a little.

What could that be, she wondered? She knew she hadn't seen it before and she had looked at that fence every day and night for years. The clouds covered the moon again and the yard went dark. She felt prickly all over with fear at the thought of something out in the yard that she didn't recognize.

After a few minutes, the clouds uncovered the moon and the bright moonlight filled the yard again. Puddles leaned close to the window and peered out, staring hard at the fence where she had seen the mysterious shadow.

She caught her breath and her hand went up automatically to cover her mouth. She drew back from the window. The shadow looked like a monster! It was big and it was shaped like some of the monsters she had seen in books and on television. The impression was that of a four-legged creature with a high back and a large snout.

She leaned near the window again and took another look. She tried hard to connect the monster to something she had seen before. It wasn't exactly a wolf, but it did seem like some kind of dog-like creature ... if only she could remember.

Wait! Maybe she did know! In her mind she could see the creature, but she had to think hard for the name. H-m-m-m, she thought, it was something she had definitely seen ... it was ... it was something like a ... h-m-m-m, maybe a Chupacabra, or something like that. It was a monster! She thought that it was from South

America – and she knew that it attacks people and it drinks blood! She was afraid.

What's it doing here? She couldn't understand why it would be out in her backyard! Could it get into the house? Could it climb, she wondered? Could it actually climb up to her window?

She was petrified with fear. She couldn't look away. Every time the clouds uncovered the moon she could see the monster's shadow on the fence. There it was! There was no doubt about it, and it was in her yard! She wanted to scream but she didn't want to get the monster's attention by yelling out.

While she was staring at the shadow on the fence, and trying to decide what she should do, a voice behind her made her jump straight up out of her chair!

"My heavens," her mother said from the doorway, "what are you doing?"

"Oh, Mother, you scared me almost to death!" Puddles answered. She could feel her heart racing and her breath was coming in quick gasps.

"Puddles, whatever are you talking about?" her mother asked.

"There's a monster out in the backyard!" Puddles declared.

"What kind of monster?" her mother asked. "What would a monster be doing out there?"

"Oh, Mother, it's a Chupacabra!" Puddles said frighteningly. "It's out in the yard! I can see the shadow on the fence. And … it drinks blood!

"Oh, good gracious," her mother responded. "How would something like that get into the yard?"

"I don't know, but it's there," Puddles said. "You can look for yourself."

Her mother came over to the window.

"Watch the back fence by the tree," Puddles instructed. "When the moon moves out from behind the clouds, you'll see it; it's right there."

Her mother leaned close to the window. When the yard lit up with moonlight, she caught her breath.

"See? I told you," Puddles said.

Her mother kept watching through the window. After see saw the shadow a second time, she let out a sigh of relief.

"See?" Aren't you scared, Mother?" Puddles was confused that her mother didn't seem frightened.

"Come look," her mother said, motioning her over to the window. "Let me show you something."

Puddles hesitantly stepped toward the window.

"I want you to look at the tree in front of the fence," her mother said.

Puddles waited for the clouds to move from in front of the moon. She was looking at the tree when the moonlight washed across the yard.

"See?" her mother said. "Do you see it?"

"Yes ... yes, I do," Puddles breathed loudly. "The monster is up in the tree!"

"Look closely," her mother said, as she put her finger on the glass. "It's a raccoon. It's in the tree. The brightness of the moon is casting a shadow on the fence that is much larger that the raccoon." She turned her face toward her daughter.

Puddles was a little hesitant to accept that. She was doubtful because she had seen the monster's shadow on the fence for herself. She leaned close to the glass and looked where her mother was pointing.

"See what I mean?" her mother asked. "When the light is behind an object, it casts a larger shadow. It's only the raccoon. The shadow is distorted. It makes it look much bigger than it really is."

Puddles looked … at the fence, at the shadow on it, and at the raccoon up in the tree. What her mother said made sense. She could see that it was true. She was *so* relieved. She would pay closer attention in the future, but nothing would ever keep her from watching the rain and the clouds.

The End

It was a dark and stormy night ...

Quinn

Quinn woke up with a start! He almost jumped up out of the chair! The sudden flash of lightning and the loud roar of thunder awakened him instantly. For a minute he wasn't sure where he was. He looked around the room. He didn't recognize the place at first. He blinked his sleepy eyes and shook his head to clear the cobwebs in there. It took him a moment to get his bearings. Oh, yeah, he was in the study at his grandparents' house. It all came back to him.

The past month had been a dizzy whirlwind of activity, but it had been fun. There had been many changes for him to get used to. He graduated from college with his teaching degree. Then, his mother told her dad that Quinn was ready to look for a teaching job somewhere.

His grandfather invited him to come to Memphis, Tennessee where he was a professor at the university. His grandpa had some connections with the local high schools and he got Quinn an interview.

Quinn drove across the country alone. It was his biggest adventure, so far. He got the job and he was very excited about his new position. He was now 'officially' a high school history teacher. Quinn loved everything about history. He had loved the subject ever since he was a little kid. He always wanted to be a teacher – and now he was!

The past month had been really busy. Memphis was a major city. It was a huge, busy place. He knew that it would take some time to get used to. He had moved from Spokane, Washington. That was a much smaller city and he wasn't used to all the traffic in a big city like Memphis.

The busy traffic reminded him of Seattle in the mornings and the afternoons that they had run into when his family visited there. It was a nightmare. He didn't understand how the people coped with the traffic jams.

He wasn't very fond of traffic. Ever since he started driving when he was sixteen, heavy traffic had always made him nervous. But, he figured he could get used to it. It was now a part of his new life. He decided to try and look at it as part of a great new adventure.

Another thing he would have to adjust to would be his new job. Creating a curriculum for his classes and then making sure he followed it might be a great challenge for him. He knew he had a tendency to get going on a topic and ramble on and on. That's what happened during his student teaching job that he was required to do for graduation.

Quinn wondered about how to tackle the task of teaching. He had read some books about it and his teachers had talked about it in class, but he wasn't sure yet. They all said to try different ways until you find a way that suits you best.

He would have to get use to interacting with the other faculty members and the students too. After all, he was no longer one of the students – he was the actual teacher. The new role was a bit scary at first. It was like a role reversal and it was strange.

He was trying to get the students to like history, or at least be interested in it. But, Quinn knew that not everyone loved history like he did. He knew that most people thought history was boring. Other people didn't see history the way he did, as exciting adventures that had happened down through the ages.

He had thought about different ways to present the subject so that the students would pay attention and want to learn about it. He knew that most of the students were only there because the class was a required course. Well, it was a work in progress.

His grandparents had invited him to stay with them at their house in the country outside of the city. They lived in Stanton, Tennessee, which was about forty miles outside of Memphis. He was glad to be away from the hustle and the bustle of the city when he got off work in the afternoons. At least school let out a couple of hours before the afternoon traffic started. He was very happy about that.

Quinn loved the quietness of the area and the sounds of the birds and other things that you couldn't really hear in the city with all the noise. His grandparents had ten acres of forest behind their house and he loved walking around in the woods.

Suddenly, a flash of lightning broke into his thoughts. Then, the boom of thunder bellowed loudly over the house and it was almost deafening. Wow, they sure have some severe storms here, he thought. That was something else he would have to get used to in his new life.

Grandpa said they sometimes get tornados in the area. Quinn had never seen a tornado. He thought that it might be kind of cool to see, but his grandparents promised him that once he saw one, he'd be cured of the fascination. That was why they had a storm shelter in the backyard. It was dug deep into the ground and it had a strong door covering it.

Quinn had never seen a storm shelter either. Grandpa told him that everyone in the area had a shelter on their property. He wondered why it wasn't in the basement under the house. Grandpa said that you don't want a shelter under the house because the house could be knocked down during a tornado and everyone could be trapped underneath it.

He was in his grandpa's study. It looked like a library to him. His grandpa called it his 'sanctuary' and he had his quiet time there. It was a place for him to gather his thoughts, he said. Grandpa gave him permission to go in at any time and read the books. To get away from the world outside, Quinn liked sitting in the big easy chair and reading the books from the shelves. He knew that this could easily become a habit for him. He kind of looked at the study as his sanctuary too.

Another bright flash of lightning lit up the room and a big roar of thunder rumbled across the sky. In the lightning he could see the trees light up in the backyard through the windows and double doors of the study. He noticed that it was dark outside.

There had been no storm in the afternoon when he came in to read for a while. He must have fallen asleep. He looked around the room. He was starting to get familiar with the furniture and things in there.

His grandmother had decorated the rest of the house, but his grandfather had taken over this room. It was filled with the things he loved: books, statues, pictures, and even some deer antlers on the wall that he got in Wyoming when he visited there one year on summer vacation. The people there explained that the deer shed their antlers every year and then grew new ones. That was surprising to him, grandpa said, to think that the animals could grow those big antlers back so quickly year after year.

Quinn was considering whether to go back to reading his book and picking up where he left off back when he had fallen asleep, or whether he should go to the kitchen and get something to eat. He looked down at the book.

The lights in the study blinked when the next flash of lightning lit up everything. It was funny he didn't remember the lights being on in the afternoon when he came in here. One of his grandparents must have come in and turned them on. They must have tip toed in and out, because he hadn't heard a thing. He figured he must have slept pretty soundly.

At the next flash of lightning, the lights in the room flickered and then they went out. He sat still. He remembered his grandmother said that the power was subject to Mother Nature's whims and when they went out they usually came back on after a few minutes. She said they were rarely off more than an hour or so. It didn't seem to bother either one of them that the electricity went out sometimes.

Quinn decided that he would just relax and wait out the storm – and the power outage. He sat in the big chair and watched the trees in the backyard light up with each lightning flash. He could see the rain coming down pretty good out in the yard.

Wait! He noticed something when the lightning flashed. He turned to look at grandpa's desk. There was a two-foot tall, black ceramic statue of a jaguar sitting on the far corner of the desk.

The jaguar was posed like it was sneaking along after something, ready to pounce. There were red stones in its eyes. It looked kind of real. Grandpa said he picked it up in China when he traveled there while he was in the military. When the lightning lit up the room, the cat's eyes glittered and glowed bright red. Quinn turned back to watching the storm outside.

After a few lightning flashes and booms of thunder, he turned to look at the jaguar again. The glowing eyes seemed to be closer! Nah ... that must be his imagination, he thought to himself. The statue was *not* moving, he told himself! He tried to convince himself – NO way in this world is that jaguar moving closer, he said inside his head! That's just so silly. What an imagination. His mother always said he had an overactive imagination. He hadn't really thought about that until now.

After a few minutes, he decided to look at the jaguar again. He was almost certain that it was closer. The glittering eyes were staring at him in the lightning flashes and it was definitely closer than it had been before. No ... no way – he didn't want to believe it! He couldn't understand how the cat could be closer.

But, I can see it, he said to himself! He couldn't talk himself out of the notion that the jaguar was slowly moving toward him. The very idea of it moving was ridiculous, he told himself. It's a ceramic statue! He didn't believe that it could move – he wouldn't believe it – not for a minute. It's impossible!

"That is the silliest thing you've ever come up with," he said out loud.

Whether it was a dumb idea or not he was sitting there looking at it with his own eyes. He could see it! In the next lightning flash he saw the jaguar was even closer. Now ... he was sure. It was supposed to be over there on the far end of the desk. Now it was most of the way over to this side. Wait! It was crossing the desk toward him a little at a time – no doubt about it!

Quinn was frightened. This was getting spooky, he thought. He decided that the jaguar must be cursed or something because he was convinced that it was moving. It was moving across his grandpa's desk all on its own.

He was starting to feel more afraid. He decided he wasn't about to keep sitting there and wait for the big cat to reach the end of the desk and jump on him.

He put his hands on the arms of the chair and braced himself to jump up and run. The book that was lying on his lap slipped off onto the floor, but he didn't notice it. He was closely watching the desk.

The next flash of lightning came and the jaguar was just about to the end of the desk! He looked away from the cat. Quinn gripped the arms of the chair with his hands and he got ready to move. He took a deep breath and let it out slowly. He jumped up, and ran for the door.

Suddenly the lights came back on! He ran straight into his grandpa in the doorway. He almost knocked him down. The sudden appearance of his grandfather just about gave him a heart attack. He grabbed his chest and let out a little sound. He looked back toward the desk and scooted around behind his grandfather.

"What's going on in here?" Grandpa asked.

Quinn put his hands on his grandpa's shoulders and peered over his right shoulder.

"What are you doing?" Grandpa asked.

"That cat on the desk!" he gasped. "It was moving! It was coming toward me!"

"Nonsense," Grandpa answered.

"No, really," Quinn wheezed, "it's possessed or something! It was trying to jump on me."

His grandfather chuckled. "That old statue can't hurt you," he said.

"But, I saw it!" Quinn exclaimed. "It was moving! It was after me! It almost jumped on me in the dark!

"Oh, that," Grandpa said.

"What do you mean?" Quinn asked.

"Well," Grandpa added, "I forgot to mention that the leg on that old desk is broken."

"The leg on the desk is broken?" Quinn asked. He was confused about what the leg of the desk had to do with the possessed jaguar. "What does that mean? How does that matter?"

"I've been meaning to get it fixed," Grandpa explained. "I haven't seemed to get around to it yet. I guess I'm just used to it by now. The broken desk makes the desk lean a little. When the lightning and thunder come with the storms, the vibration of the storm shakes the desk a little and the cat glides across the top a little at a time. At some point it reaches the end of the desk if the storm lasts a long time. I was just coming in here to catch it and move it before it fell off the desk."

"Oh, my goodness," Quinn said, breathlessly. "It kind of scared me."

"Yes, I could see that," Grandpa answered, and he chuckled again.

"Why don't you just move it away and put it somewhere else?" Quinn asked.

"Oh, it's been there forever," Grandpa explained. "I'm so used to it there that I can't seem to move it to a shelf. It's like an old friend and it keeps me company when I'm in here."

"Well, I'm glad you finally told me," Quinn said. "I thought I was about to get attacked."

"Yes, I could see that too," Grandpa said, and he chuckled one more time.

The End

Ricky

It was summertime and seven year old Ricky was visiting his grandparents on their farm. He loved being on the farm, that is, he loved it during the day. It was great fun. But, when it got dark he would start to worry. A witch lived in the forest behind the house. She would come out at night and he was afraid of her. Ricky had seen her, moving from tree to tree out in the dark forest. He could see her in the moonlight, silently gliding among the trees. It was a really scary sight and it frightened him.

Every night, before he went to bed, he would stand at the window in his bedroom and watch for the witch. He wanted to be sure she wasn't coming near the house before he went to sleep. He didn't think he would be able to sleep if she was out there flying around the house. When he saw her he would duck down so she wouldn't see him at the window. Once he was satisfied that she wasn't coming close to the house, he would go to bed.

Tonight, there was a storm. It rained hard earlier, but the rain had stopped. There was still lightning, but the thunder that was so scary had moved away. Ricky could hear it from time to time rumbling in the distance.

The rain was dripping off the edge of the roof in front of his window, but he could still see the dark forest across the backyard. And there was the mist from the river that ran through the forest. It was floating around in the trees and that made it even harder to see what was going on out there.

The dark, black clouds blocked out the moon, so there was no moonlight to help him see. Ricky was worried that the witch would be out there and he wouldn't be able to track her. The only time he could see anything was when the lightning lit up the yard. The lightning came from time to time but it was so quick and so weak that it didn't really help much.

Most nights he would spot her and he would try to look away, but he felt like he was hypnotized and he was fascinated at the same time. He just couldn't make himself stop staring. It would take him several minutes to find the strength to make his eyes blink so he could turn away from the window.

After all, he thought, you don't see a real witch every day. So far, he hadn't seen her fly toward the house. He hoped that she was satisfied staying out there in the trees. Then, in a flash of lightning, he saw her! The witch flew across in front of the trees and stopped in a treetop. He had hoped that, because there was a storm, she wouldn't be out but, there she was – just like all the other nights!

As Ricky watched, the dark shadow of the witch flew to another tree! He ducked down and peeked over the window ledge. He couldn't look away and he could feel the scary creepies coming up from his legs to cover his body.

Wait! The witch, suddenly, without any warning, flew straight toward him! As she came closer to the window, she swooped up and landed on the roof above the window!

He was horrified! He dropped flat on the floor and crawled away from the window. He scooted around the foot of the bed and hid. He was scared to death! He thought that if the witch came through the window, he was going to start crying. He could feel his eyes stinging already. Facing a witch was going to be the scariest thing he'd ever had to do.

Ricky wasn't sure what he should do. His ears were buzzing and he was having trouble thinking straight. He was too scared to crawl to the door across the room. The witch might see him and come in through the window.

As he was hiding there at the end of the bed, too afraid to move, the door suddenly opened. He almost jumped out of his skin. He looked up and he saw Grandma Verne standing in the doorway.

"I brought you some warm milk and nice cookies to have before ----," she said and stopped short when she saw him cringing on the floor at the foot of the bed.

He stared at her with his eyes opened wide in fright. He couldn't speak.

"Land sakes, Child," she said, "what on earth are you doing down there?"

"There's a witch out there," Ricky said, and his voice was shaky. "She flew at me and she landed on the roof right above the window!"

"Oh, Child, there's no witch out there," Grandma Verne said. Her voice was soothing and Ricky felt a teeny bit better.

"Yes, there is," he said. "I saw her. She was big and she's on the roof *right now!*"

"What's giving you this idea?" she asked. She put the tray she was carrying down on the bed and helped him to his feet. "Come on over here."

"Uncle John said it's a witch and that she turns little boys into donkeys," Ricky answered.

"That can't happen," Grandma Verne said.

"Yeah, I saw it in a movie," Ricky explained. "The boys were turned into donkeys. Uncle John said it was a witch that did it."

"You just come over here and sit on the bed," Grandma Verne directed. "Drink this warm milk. It'll settle you down. And eat these cookies I baked this afternoon."

"Okay," Ricky said, as he sat down next to her on the bed.

"Let me tell you a little story," Grandma Verne said. "There really is no witch. Your Uncle John is always telling some kind of story."

She put her arm around Ricky and patted him on the shoulder. He could feel that she was warm and it made him feel better.

"He told your cousin, Luke, that witches turn little boys into toads," Grandma Verne said. "Now, he's told you something different."

"Yeah," Ricky said, "he took me out to the barn to see the donkeys. He said they all have names because they were neighborhood boys the witch turned into donkeys and they came to live here."

"Look here, Child," she said, "those are the same little donkeys we had last year when you were here and they are the same little donkeys we've had since before you were born. We've had those critters for more than ten years and they've had names ever since we got them. Your Uncle John named them the day they arrived here on the farm. They're donkeys, and they've always been donkeys."

"Oh," Ricky said. Could it be true, he wondered?

"Your Uncle John is just playing a joke," she said. "He told your cousin, Heather, that the witch turns little girls into ducks. He took her out there and named them for her. Then, when your cousin, Sharon, was here, he told her the same thing. Except, he forgot the names he told Heather and so he had to make up new names. The girls got together and compared stories. That's how they found out he made up the whole thing just to play a joke on them. He's making up another story for you. There's no witch out there; it's just in Uncle John's head."

"Is that for real?" Ricky asked.

"You can bet on it," Grandma Verne said. "There's no such thing as a witch who can turn people into something else. Believe me, it's just a big old owl out there. He's been living in those trees for years. He's a real big bird and he looks really dark when he's flying around. He's only out at night because that's when he eats. During the day he's asleep, so you never see him. Uncle John knows that, so he uses him for his farfetched stories. There's not one thing out there that can hurt you. Your grandpa has talked to Uncle John about his stories before, but he just has too much fun telling them for him to stop."

"I feel better," Ricky said. "I was scared."

"C'mon," Grandma Verne said, "let's get you snuggled down under those quilts for a good night's sleep. Now, don't you go believing any more of your Uncle John's stories. They're just tall tales."

The End

It was a dark and stormy night ...

Stacy

Stacy was so excited to be at college. She had been looking forward to going for two years, ever since she accepted the academic scholarship they offered back when she started the eleventh grade.

She wanted to study veterinary medicine, with the hopes of being a veterinarian in the area where she grew up. She had always loved the animals around the farm. The veterinarian in her town, Doc Chester, told her that he would be delighted to welcome her into his practice when she graduated.

"You can't have too many doctors looking out for those critters," he said.

The prospect of having a job waiting for her when she finished college made her more excited, if that was even possible.

The college was an older school, established sometime way back in the 1890s. And, it was perfect for her, not too far from home, yet far enough away so that she would miss her family.

Stacy looked forward to the chance of making new friends. She was from a small farming town and there just weren't *that* many people her age around while she was growing up.

When she arrived at school, she was assigned a dormitory room on the second floor of an older brick building. The upstairs hallway had eight rooms, four on each side of the hall. She was so happy to meet the other girls who would live in the dorm hallway with her.

Across the hall, counting from the stairway, there was Diana, then Cora, then Heaven, and in the last room was Gwen. On Stacy's side of the hall there was Tia across from Diana and Maria across from Cora. Stacy's room was across from Heaven's room and last on her side of the hallway, across from Gwen was Cleo.

Cleo was Stacy's favorite. She had a dramatic flair the other girls didn't seem to have. She said she was named after Cleopatra and she appeared determined to be just as remarkable and theatrical as Cleopatra was in the books that Stacy had read. Stacy loved watching her in all her splendor whenever she talked. Yet, she seemed so sensible and down to earth.

Stacy was delighted with her room. It was cozy and charming. The bed was an old four-poster with a canopy, just like she had seen in old movies. There was a vanity where she could sit and brush her hair in the mirror and there was a small fireplace that hadn't been used in years.

And she loved the small balcony where she could look out over the campus. There were huge old trees everywhere and green grass and flower beds. She could smell the lavender flowers all the way up to her room when the glass door to the balcony was open. She also loved the fresh air and the openness of the college campus.

She had to share the bathroom at the end of the hall with all the other girls on the second floor, but it wasn't anything she wasn't used to. She had two sisters and two brothers back home that she shared a bathroom with her whole life.

So far, the whole experience seemed like a dream. Everything was wonderful and fascinating. Stacy had never been away from home except for a couple of trips to summer camp back when she was younger. When she told that to the other girls at her 'welcome-to-college' party, they thought she was kidding.

After being at college for just a couple of days, a storm rose up out of the west and swept across the area. The thunder and lightning were unnerving. She had been through many storms before, but she had been at home, in the comfort and security of her familiar bedroom.

Now, in this new place, the storm made her feel a little anxious. The view of the campus from the balcony door was all distorted because of the rain that was blown against the glass by the wind and clung there, refusing to run down like she expected that it should. She looked out through the rain drops sticking to the window and the area looked spooky and unreal.

Stacy closed the drapes so that she wouldn't feel uneasy every time she looked out. After dinner she settled down at the small writing desk to read an assignment she was given in her history class. As she became more involved in reading the book, trying to remember facts and dates, in case there was a test, she kind of blocked out the storm and the rain that was lashing against the glass of the door to the balcony. As she was reading, the lights suddenly went out when a boom of thunder shook the building.

The room was thrown into darkness! The lamp on the desk was the only light she had on. She thought perhaps the bulb burned out. She tried turning the lamp off and on but it was no use – it wasn't going to work. She didn't have a spare bulb. She made a mental note to ask for a new bulb the next day.

She went across the room and flipped the light switch on the wall next to the door leading out into the hall. Nothing happened. She flipped the switch again but the room remained pitch dark. With the drapes closed there was absolutely no light in the room.

Stacy opened her door and looked out into the hall. The hall lights were on. That was weird. How could the lights be out in her room, while the hall lights remained on? She closed the door and leaned against it. She wondered what she should do. She looked at her wristwatch. It was eleven o'clock. She didn't want to wake up anyone at that hour.

Suddenly, there was a flash of lightning and another crash of thunder. The bright flash of lightning told her that the storm was directly over the campus. As the flash of light brightened the room she looked across at the balcony door.

Wait! There was the shadow of a man on the drapes! Stacy thought her heart stopped with the shock. Why was a man on her balcony? She could clearly see his outline on the drapes. He was standing outside the door. How could he get up there? She thought he could probably climb up from the patio that was directly below her balcony.

Her heart started beating frantically. She was afraid to move. What should she do? Standing there in the darkness too petrified to even move, she was confused. She suddenly couldn't think straight. Her mind seems muddled and her thoughts were blurry. She had always been so calm and so level-headed. It was all so strange to her.

The idea of fleeing jumped into her head. Yes, she had to get out of there! She reached out her hand until it touched the dresser along the wall next to the door. She knew her purse was there with her car keys in it. She felt around and finally located it.

Stacy quietly picked up her purse, all the while keeping her eyes on the shadow at the balcony door. She softly opened the door to the hall and slipped out. She stood in the lighted hallway for a few moments.

The lights in the hall made everything seem so much better. The hall was quiet. All the girls must be asleep, she thought. She tip toed down the hallway to the stairs, trying not to wake anyone who might be asleep. She went silently down the steps and paused on the first floor. Everything was very quiet down there also.

Suddenly, a boom of thunder frightened her. She jumped and ran for the front door. She ran out the door, across the porch, and across the driveway to her car. She pressed the button on her key fob to unlock the door as she ran. She jumped into the car, slammed the door, and locked all the doors.

After sitting for a few minutes and catching her breath, Stacy realized that perhaps she should have stayed inside the building and gotten help there, but she had been so scared. She didn't want to disturb the other girls and let them see that she was afraid.

Since she had told them this was her first time away from home, she didn't want to be the big baby in the dorm who missed her mother, who was afraid of being away from home, and who was afraid of the storm. She would be so embarrassed and they might tease her about it for the whole school year.

No, she decided, she was better off in her car. She felt safe there. Besides, she could always drive away if something were to happen. She reached into the back seat and got the blanket she always kept there. She covered herself up with the blanket and settled down to wait ... for what, she wasn't sure ... until when, she wasn't sure of that either.

At some point she fell asleep. She woke up to the sun shining in through the windshield and hitting her right in the face as it rose over the trees. The storm had passed. She blinked her eyes and looked around, wondering where she was.

Then, it all came back to her – the man on her balcony! She remembered. She looked down at her wristwatch and saw that it was seven o'clock. She got out of the car and went into the building.

In the upstairs hall she ran into Cleo.

"What are you doing out here? I knocked on your door but I didn't get an answer," she said.

Stacy quickly thought up an excuse for being outside so early. "Oh, I went for a little walk," Stacy explained.

Cleo looked surprised. She said, "You went for a walk in your pajamas?"

Stacy looked down and realized that she was indeed wearing her pajamas. "Oh, that's why I have this blanket," she answered, indicating the blanket wrapped around her shoulders. She wasn't sure Cleo believed her story.

"Well, okay, then," Cleo said. "We've got school in two hours – be there or be square." She smiled.

Stacy went into her room. The first thing she did was flip the light switch. The lights came on. She went over and tried the lamp. That worked fine also. She hesitantly went over to the drapes and peeked out onto the balcony. It was empty. She opened the drapes, opened the door, and went out.

She looked around, but nothing appeared to be out of place. Everything seemed just ordinary. There were no signs that anyone had been out there. There were no footprints. She wasn't sure what she was looking for, but whatever it was, she was glad she didn't find it. She went back inside and got ready for class.

She had such a good day that she forgot all about her terrifying episode of the night before. If she had thought about it, she probably would have chalked it up to her imagination.

In the late afternoon, the storm rolled back into the area from the east. Stacy figured it was the same storm and it had decided to go back the way it had come from the night before. But, the sunshine during the day had been welcome.

After dinner she settled into her room. While she was reading one of her schoolbooks, the lights suddenly went out again! Oh, no, she thought. Suddenly, there was the lightning which made her jump in surprise.

The lightning was followed instantly by the thunder. She looked quickly at the balcony door and, in the flash of lightning she saw the man's shadow reflected on the drapes. He was back! He was standing right outside the door! She watched the shadow and suddenly it moved!

She couldn't help herself – she screamed without meaning to … it just happened. Suddenly, there was the sound of running feet. Her door burst open and there was Cleo, Maria, and Heaven in the doorway. Cleo was carrying a flashlight. She shined it at Stacy.

Maria leaned back out into the hallway and yelled toward the stairway, "Cheryl! Cheryl!" In just a minute the lights came back on.

"What on earth are you screaming for, girl," Cleo asked plainly.

"There's a man on my balcony," Stacy explained. "He's right outside the glass door. I saw him in the lightning when the lights went out."

Cleo marched over to the balcony door and flung back the drapes. Stacy was shocked that she didn't appear to be one bit afraid.

"Nope, no one there," Cleo said matter-of-factly.

"But, I'm sure I saw him," Stacy argued.

Cleo looked around. "No way," she said. "Ain't no dude going to get up here."

"But, I saw him," Stacy said.

"Well," Cleo started, "let me tell you what's really going on here. I know, maybe we should have told you about it, but I guess nobody thought of it. Here, Maria, take this flashlight and go outside on the balcony there. Heaven, you close those drapes and we'll show Stacy here what we're talking about."

Maria went outside but she left the door open. Heaven closed the drapes behind her and turned to face Stacy and Cleo.

"Now," Cleo said, "wait for the lightning and we'll see what happens."

They waited a little more than a minute. The lightning flashed and Stacy drew back – there was the man's shadow on the drapes!

"Okay," Cleo declared. Heaven opened the drapes and Maria came inside and closed the door.

"Now, come over here and have a look," Cleo said, urging Stacy toward the door. Stacy hesitated but Cleo put her arm around her and moved her over to the door.

"Watch what happens in the lightning," Cleo said. "Now you look close and you'll see just what I'm talking about."

Stacy stood still, hesitantly looking outside. The lightning flashed.

"Right there," Cleo declared. She bent forward and pointed. "Now, do you see that old tree – that one right there, the one that's all tangled and gnarly? Now watch."

She nodded at Heaven, and Heaven closed the drapes again. At the next lightning flash, Cleo pointed toward the drapes. Suddenly, at exactly the place where she pointed, the man's shadow appeared on the drapes!

Startled, Stacy asked, "What is it?"

Cleo raised her opened hands. "It's nothing," she answered. "Simple as that – when the lightning lights up out there, it makes that old tree reflect on the building. It just so happens to be right on your door there. I know it's weird, but the shadow it casts looks just like a man. When the wind blows it makes it look like he's moving too. It's weird huh?"

"Creepy," Stacy agreed.

Cleo said, "Donna, the girl who lived in here last year had the same thing happen to her. She was just about scared out of her wits. It's just that old tree. Not a thing to be scared about."

"Well, I feel better," Stacy said. She felt so relieved. She felt silly for overreacting. "It didn't occur to me that it could be something like that. I just saw a man standing there."

"Well, that's about as exciting as it gets around here," Cleo said. "No big deal."

"Oh, yeah," Heaven said, "we also forgot to tell you about the lights. This is a really, really old building. The circuit breaker for the lights on this side of the hallway is really sensitive. When there's a storm, the vibration of the thunder, when it's really loud, trips the breaker and puts out the lights."

"That's why I called for Cheryl," Maria added. "She's on the first floor and the circuit breaker is right outside her room. Any time it trips, we yell, and she flips it back on."

"If it's late at night, we just wait until morning," Heaven said, "so we don't wake anyone up just to flip the breaker. You can go down and flip it yourself if you want."

"I'd advise you to get a couple of candles," Maria said. "We've all got them."

"Oh, I'm so relieved," Stacy said.

"Well," Cleo said, "welcome to college!"

The End

It was a dark and stormy night ...

Taven and Cody

Taven and Cody were first cousins. Their fathers were brothers and they lived on farms that were only three miles apart. The boys were the same age and they were also best friends. Their parents joked that, if you see one, the other wouldn't be far behind. They teased them by calling them the inseparable twins.

Yes, they lived three miles apart, that is, if you went down the roads, they said. But, they knew they could cut the distance to only two miles if they went across the pastures and through the forest between their farms. They figured they had made that hike thousands of times.

They had been running back and forth between the two farms almost since they could walk. For years Taven's older brother would go with them to be sure they were safe. But, when they turned twelve years old, they started just going by themselves, either alone or together. Sometimes they would meet halfway between their houses.

Taven's brother had taught them how to cross the pastures without disturbing the bulls that were out there. It didn't take the boys long to learn how upset the bulls could get if they felt someone was coming into their territory. With all the open space in the fields, it was difficult to outrun the bulls and there were very few places to hide from them.

Luckily, there was usually a tree or two left out in the center of each pasture. The farmers hoped that, during a storm, the lightning would strike the trees rather than the cows that might be standing around out there. There had been several occasions where the boys were forced to climb a tree and wait until the bull chasing them went away and left them alone.

They were at Cody's house. They had been stuck in the house all day because a storm was 'racing across the valley' as Cody's dad expressed it. The boys didn't see much 'racing' to it because, if it was *racing through the area*, they felt it should have been gone a long time ago.

They were tired of the things they could do at Cody's house. Taven had video games at his house that they wanted to play and Cody didn't have the same games. They needed to go to Taven's house.

They asked Cody's father about going. He wasn't so sure they should go out into the storm, just so they could play a specific game at the other house. He didn't want them to be out walking in such bad weather. The lightning was a concern. He felt it could be dangerous.

The boys reasoned that, if the lightning struck the ground, it would strike the trees first, instead of them, because the trees were taller. They tried to explain that to Cody's father to convince him that they would be safe.

The boys assured Cody's dad that they weren't afraid of the storm, that they didn't mind getting wet from the rain, and that they promised to go straight over the fields to Taven's house without stopping. They even offered to run the whole way if it would make him feel better about letting them go, but he laughed and said that it wouldn't be necessary.

The boys had worked on their family farms since they were very young. Cody's dad knew that they were both strong, tough kids. They had been out in the rain many times while out doing chores around their farms during rain storms. His main concern was the lightning. It wasn't something to mess with.

Cows, horses, pigs, goats, chickens, and ducks, one or the other of their farms owned all of them and the boys had dealt with them all at one time or another over the years. It didn't matter whether it rained or snowed, or not, the animals still had to be tended to.

Cody's dad told them to go ahead, but he told Cody to call his uncle and let him know they were on the way, so someone could expect them and maybe watch out for them. He wasn't afraid for them. He just felt that you could never be too cautious. You never knew what could happen, especially living on farms in rural areas.

It was a little different for the kids living in town. There weren't the same dangers for them. But, there were many dangers on a farm that you had to be aware of and take precautions for. It was just a way of life and every kid living on a farm learned very early to keep an eye out and to pay attention to his surroundings. Accidents happened – especially freak accidents happened around farms and being aware of everything around you could greatly lessen the possibility of those accidents. The boys had learned to be safe, around the farm, and around the animals.

Cody called his uncle to let him know they were on the way. Taven said to tell him that they would be there within the hour. Taven's dad said he would listen for them and see them when they got there.

The boys set off in the direction of Taven's house. There would be a few fences they had to go over, but they were experts at hopping fences. They were a little surprised at how dark it was. Because of the storm and heavy black clouds, there was no moon and in the rural area, there weren't any outside lights. The only lights were the lights on at night around the farmhouses and the barns.

Also, surrounding the farms and in between some of them, there was forest. The woods were thick and the undergrowth could be dense in places. The boys had spent a lot of time in the woods over the years. They knew their way around.

You always had to be aware when you were going through the forest because there were a few wild animals out there. There were farm animals in the fields and wild animals in the woods. The boys didn't want to walk up on a wolf, or a bear. They would listen, but most of the time you couldn't hear animals approaching.

They knew that the bears and wolves lived mostly in the mountains to the west. But, occasionally they would stray down into the valley. The boys had run into them in the forest only twice in their memory.

They also knew to watch for the deer and elk. During certain seasons of the year, they could be dangerous, especially the bucks, because of their antlers. Usually, they would move away from people coming through the woods, but you could never know ahead of time how they were going to react to you coming upon them

They hopped the fence in back of the barn behind Cody's house and cut across the corner of the field toward the woods. They would cut through the forest, come out on the other side, cut across another field, then more woods, and then they would be on Taven's property. They would cross the last pasture and end up at one of the barns before reaching his house.

"Wow, it sure is dark," Cody said.

"Yeah," Taven agreed, "it's darker than I thought it would be."

"I can't see a thing," Cody said. "Should we go back? I can't see anything in the dark, especially with the rain running down my face and into my eyes."

"No, we already left," Taven said. "We don't have to go back. It's dark, but we know where we're going. We've been this way lots of times after dark. Besides, every time the lightning flashes we can see our way ahead. If we're not sure, all we have to do is wait for the next flash, and we can figure out where we are."

"What if we stop and wait for the lightning and, when it comes, we see a bear standing right in front of us?" Cody asked. "What about that? What are we going to do then?"

"That's not going to happen," Taven answered. "The bears are smart enough to get in out of the rain. I'm sure they're tucked away somewhere. Don't worry about it. We won't run into them."

"What if the lightning comes and we see a bunch of wolves surrounding us?" Cody asked. "What then? Are we just going to jump up in the air and fly away?"

"Don't be dumb," Taven said. "You've never seen a pack of wolves. We've only seen a couple and they were always alone. They didn't belong to any pack."

"I don't know, I'm thinking we should maybe go back until the storm passes over," Cody put in.

"Nah, we've come this far," Taven answered. "We might as well go on. I'm not worried about wolves."

"I think I'm a little scared," Cody said. "We should have brought flashlights."

"We don't need them," Taven answered.

"If you say so," Cody said.

"Don't be a chicken," Taven added. "I'll tell you what, if we run into a bear, I'll just wrestle it to the ground and hold it until you can get away and save yourself."

Cody laughed. "Smart Alec ... you're very funny," he said.

"Okay then," Taven said, "see how silly it sounds? There's nothing to be scared of. Have you ever met anything out here that attacked you?"

"Well, we had those bulls chasing us a few times," Cody answered back.

"Besides that," Taven said.

"Well, then, what about that dog that chased us through the woods that time?" Cody asked.

"Yeah, besides that," Taven said.

"Well, what about that skunk?"

"All right, all right, I get the point," Taven said. "Just forget I said anything."

"Okay," Cody answered, laughing. He didn't often get the better of his cousin.

"Come on," Taven said, "we'll be there before you know it."

The boys crossed fields, hopped fences, passed through the woods, hopped another fence, and they were at the edge of one of the pastures of Taven's farm. Every time the lightning flashed they would look up through the rain to get their bearings.

They could see a light by the barn behind Taven's house away across the field in the distance. They walked along a little cautiously in the dark because they knew there were some rabbit burrows in the field. There had been a couple of times when the cows stepped into one and hurt their legs.

Cody was running across the field with Taven once when they were in the fourth grade and he stepped into one of the rabbit holes and sprained his ankle. He never forgot the pain of having almost broken his ankle. He was always cautious when crossing the field. He usually watched the ground as he went along but now, in the dark, he could barely see the ground. Waiting for the lightning flashes so he could see wasn't doing much good. The flashes were too brief to really get a sense of the ground for very far in front of him.

As they crossed the pasture, they passed the tree near the center and they were about to go by the cow pond. The pond was created there so the cows could get a drink of water when they were in that field. It was a fairly large pond and it was surrounded by reeds, weeds, and cattails.

The cousins had gone swimming in the pond a number of times. The cows didn't seem to mind that the boys were dirtying up their drinking water. Taven pointed out once that the cows were standing in the water too while they were drinking. So, he said, they didn't know the difference and apparently they didn't care if the water was dirty.

The pond wasn't very deep except for an area out in the middle. Out there, it was about five feet deep but the rest of the pond was only about two or three feet deep. The animals mostly kept near the edges of the pond and didn't usually wade out very far.

Taven's dog, Snapper, could swim across from side to side, but he'd never seen any other animals do it.

As they were walking along, the lightning flashed and Cody stopped suddenly and put out his arm across in front of Taven to hold him back.

"Wait! What's that over there?" he asked quietly.

Taven looked around. "Over where?" he asked.

"Out in the pond," Cody answered.

Taven looked toward the pond. He said, "I don't see anything."

"Just wait for the lightning," Cody instructed. "Something's out in the water!"

The boys looked at the pond and waited for the lightning to light up the area. When it came, they could see a large figure out in the water a short distance from the water's edge.

Cody stepped around behind Taven, pointed over his shoulder, and asked in a whisper, "What the heck is that?"

"Maybe one of the cows," Taven answered back.

"No way, it's too big," Cody disagreed, "it's huge. Besides, didn't your dad just move the cows to the pasture on the other side of the barn yesterday?"

'You're right," Taven said. "There shouldn't be any cows in this field."

The lightning flashed again and Taven could hear the sharp intake of breath from Cody, who was just behind his ear.

"Wait! It's a swamp monster!" Cody whispered into Taven's ear. "Did you see it?"

"I saw something," Taven said, "but I didn't get a good look. I'm not sure what it is."

"No ... you didn't see, it? It was real tall and it had long hair or something and it was draped in long trailing swamp weeds, just like you see in the movies," Cody said. "It's a swamp monster, I tell you! What else looks like that?"

The lightning flashed again and Taven felt Cody's fingers digging into his shoulders from behind. That's how he knew that Cody was really scared. It was just so crazy to think a swamp monster was out here in his pond. Who would ever believe it? There weren't any swamps around here, he thought.

"See, I'm telling you, it's a swamp monster," Cody hissed in fear.

Taven could hear the fear in Cody's voice. He could feel his own fear starting to crawl up his back. He waited for a flash of light. It was fast. It was too quick to really see what he was looking at, but he decided that Cody might be right. The glimpse he got sure looked like the swamp monster they had seen in the movies.

He was feeling a little wobbly and he could feel that Cody was a little shaky too.

"See," Cody whispered, "see, I told you!"

"I think you're right," Taven whispered. "I wonder where it came from."

"Duh, who the heck cares where it came from," Cody whispered. "It's right there in your pond and I think it kidnaps people and eats them! Don't you remember the movies? It eats people, right?"

"Maybe," Taven answered. "We don't want to wait to find out!"

"Let's go get your dad before it gets away," Cody suggested.

"Okay," Taven agreed. "Just back away slowly," he directed. "Don't make a sound."

The boys backed away for a distance. When they felt they were out of earshot of the swamp creature, they started running. They reached the house, out of breath and scared half to death.

As the boys ran into the house, Taven yelled, "Dad, Dad!"

"Whoa ... whoa there fellas," his dad responded, jumping up from his chair. "Is the sky falling out there, Chicken Little?"

"No, Uncle Joe," Cody exclaimed. "There's a swamp monster out there in the pond! I thought it was going to attack us!"

"A swamp monster, you say," his uncle replied, and he sounded doubtful.

"No, really, Dad," Taven put in, "it was huge and it wanted to kidnap us. You might never have seen us again!"

"How unfortunate," his dad replied, and he still sounded like he wasn't sure he should believe them. "That would be a tragedy." He looked like he was holding back his laughter.

"No really, Uncle Joe, it's true. It was a swamp monster," Cody added. "We saw it looking at us. It was right there at the edge of the pond. You have to do something!"

Taven's dad smiled and said, "Okay, let's go see this monster of yours. Are you sure it's not a wolf or something?"

"No, Dad, it's too big for that," Taven said. "It's a swamp monster, like I said. We saw it!"

"Let me get my gun," his dad said. "It's probably a wolf. A shot up in the air should scare it off the property."

He took his gun from the rack above the fireplace. He opened a drawer on a table in the hall and handed the boys each a flashlight. He turned and followed the boys out the door.

As they approached the pond, the boys hung back a little way. The flashlights remained dark in their hands. In their fear they forgot they were even carrying them.

Taven's dad cautiously approached the pond while the boys got ready to run. He stopped just before the pond and waited for the lightning flash. He didn't have to wait very long. The flash lit up the pond and then everything was dark again.

Just a minute later, Taven's dad came walking back to them. He didn't appear to be afraid at all. He sure seemed calm for someone who had just seen a swamp monster standing in his pond.

"What is it, Dad?" Taven asked. "Did you see it? You didn't shoot the gun."

"It wasn't necessary," his dad replied.

"Was it still there?" Cody asked. "Did you see it? Was it gone already?"

"Yes, I mean, no," he answered. "I mean yes, I saw it and no, it wasn't gone."

"Was it big?" Taven asked. "Did you scare it away?"

"There was no need to scare it away," he said.

"What do you mean?" Cody asked. "Are you going to let it live in the pond and eat the cows?"

"Look here boys, calm down," he said. "You both have flashlights. Shine them over there on your swamp monster."

The boys hesitated. They didn't want to see the swamp creature in the light.

Taven's dad took his flashlight from him and pointed it toward the pond. "Look at this," he said. He turned it on and moved it until it lit up the creature.

"What is it?" Taven asked quietly.

Cody moved up closer so that he could see where his uncle was pointing the light.

"It's only an elk," his dad answered. "It's wet from the rain and muddy from being in the pond. It has grass and reeds tangled up in its antlers from going through the weeds. In the dark it looks swampy, I guess, but as you can see, it's just getting a drink. You just saw it from the front so it looked like a two-legged creature. If you had seen it from the side, I'm sure you would have recognized it right away."

"We sure thought it was a swamp creature," Taven said.

"Yeah," Cody said, "it sure looked like a monster."

His Uncle Joe said, "The storm and the lightning just spooked you. That's all." He placed his hand on Cody's shoulder and patted him a couple of times. "Out on a night without a moon, it's easy to let your imagination get the better of you," he added.

"We were scared," Cody said.

"C'mon, you two," Taven's dad said, "let's get back to the house and get you out of those wet clothes." He smiled and turned back toward the house.

The boys looked at each other, but they didn't say anything. They smiled foolishly and they turned back toward the house too.

The End

Uh-oh!

Timothy was such a jokester. He had three older sisters and he just loved to play tricks on them. He said it was to get even with them for treating him like a baby. His defense was that it wasn't his fault he was born last. And, not only was he born last, but the sister closest to him in age was more than five years older than he was.

He played his jokes and it always seemed like he would get caught right away. Somehow, everyone knew immediately that it was him. He didn't quite understand how they always knew, but they did. When he got caught, he always said, "Uh-oh." He had said it ever since he was little. He had said it so many times that his sisters started calling him *Little Uh-oh*.

It took a while to get used to that. But, he figured that being 'Little Uh-oh' was a lot better than being a baby. After all, he boasted, he *was* eight years old on his last birthday and that was a long way from being a baby.

He would say he was 'practically a teenager' and his sisters would laugh and say that him being a teenager was a really, *really* long way off.

He knew that his sisters, Tami, Tayla, and Teddi were right, but he wasn't about to admit that to any one of them. But, it did seem like an awfully long time between birthdays.

In the meantime, while Timothy was waiting to be a teenager, he felt that he had a duty, as the only boy in the family, to keep it lively. And he did.

He played jokes on his sisters anytime he could think of something really cool to do. He wasn't certain, but sometimes his tricks didn't work and he had a tiny suspicion that they knew beforehand when he was about to play the trick.

Timothy was *very* careful to be sure his sisters weren't following him and spying on him while he was making all of his preparations. But, even though he had been extra, extra careful, he still suspected that somehow, some way, they always seem to know what he was up to.

It was really disappointing when he sprang his trick and they weren't surprised, or scared, or whatever effect he thought the trick would produce.

His sisters said they had a crystal ball that told them what he was going to do. They told him that he should stop all his tricks because they would always, always know what he was planning.

When Timothy said he didn't believe them, they would laugh and laugh. He didn't think it could be true because some of the time his jokes worked great. He would challenge them to show him the crystal ball to prove it was true, but they said they weren't falling for that trick. They said they didn't have to prove anything, that it was their secret, and they weren't about to let him in on their secret.

Because he didn't believe what they were saying was true, he snuck into their rooms and looked around for their crystal ball when they weren't there. He didn't find it.

He asked his mother about it, but she didn't know. She said she didn't know about a crystal ball, but that maybe a little bird was telling them. He thought that sounded more farfetched that the crystal ball, that is, until the next morning when he saw a little bird, outside on his window ledge, looking into his room. Then, the next day it was back. It was there every morning for a couple of weeks.

Then, Timothy asked his mother about it one morning at breakfast. His sisters all burst out laughing. Their mother looked sternly at them and they stopped laughing. She told the girls to confess. She knew something was going on and that they were behind it somehow.

They did confess. Teddi said that she heard their mother tell him about the little bird keeping an eye on him and tattling about what it saw. That gave the girls a great idea on how to play a trick on him. They thought they would turn the tables on him and play their own joke.

So, they would sneak into his room every night after he went to sleep and they put bird seed outside on his window ledge so that the birds would come and sit in front of his window every morning. They said that he almost woke up once, but that they were very quiet. They felt it was a great joke, but Timothy couldn't quite see the humor.

It was so much better when it was one of *his* jokes. He had some really good ones over the past couple of years. The time he waited in the kitchen cabinet for one of them to open it so he could surprise them. That was a good one.

Or the time he waited in the shower with the curtain closed for what seemed like a hundred hours for one of them to come along so he could scare them. But, it was his father who came along and spoiled it. Okay, so, that one didn't work ... but it would have been a good idea if it *had* worked.

A better one was the time he took the straw scarecrow from his mother's garden and put it on a long bean pole. He and his friend, Scotty, lifted the pole so that the scarecrow was looking into Tami's window. Wow, he thought, that one was really cool. You could hear her scream all over the neighborhood. Yeah ... that was one of his best jokes ever.

Then, there was the time that he put the Halloween mask on Georgie, their dog, and had him sit in front of Tayla's door until she opened it. He finally had to tap on the door to get her to come out. That scream was okay, it was good, but nothing matched the scarecrow scream. He wished he had recorded that one.

Timothy's mother and father called their house a *very efficient household*, which, his mother explained, meant that everybody did what they were supposed to do around the house.

In the kitchen there was a chart hanging on the wall. It listed all of the chores that needed to be done around the house, who was supposed to do them, and when the chores were to be done. His sisters took turns loading the dishwasher, running the vacuum, dusting the book shelves in the living room, and a bunch of other stuff. Each sister also did her own laundry.

Timothy had to take out the trash, bring in the mail, sweep the porch and sidewalk leading up to the house, and keep his room cleaned at all times.

That's how they got their allowance each week. When the chart showed that their chores had been done, they would get half of their money – the other half went into their savings accounts.

Both of their parents worked so the kids had to help out around the house. It had always been that way. Their parents said that having chores helped them have a good work ethic and that it made everyone responsible for something.

Their father was a doctor. Sometimes he had to go to the hospital at a moment's notice when he was needed for surgery. He would jump up and rush out anytime that his pager went off.

Their mother was a judge in what the family called *kid's court*. As the judge, she would decide when the cases would begin in her courtroom. She scheduled the cases for after her children went to school and she would stop so she could be home when they got out of school. She dropped Timothy off at school in the morning and she drove by his school in the afternoon to pick him up.

His oldest sister, Tami, drove her own car so all three sisters rode together to school every day. When the sisters played sports, they were responsible for their own transportation. Sometimes Tami would take them and pick them up and other times they would get a ride with the parents of friends who were also playing sports.

One day, Timothy was down in the basement with his dad, watching him put a bookshelf together when he got a great new idea. He didn't usually go down into the basement because it was spooky down there. But while he was there, the new idea came to him.

In the corner, under the stairs that led down into the basement, there were two big trunks. They had been there his whole life but he never paid much attention to them.

His father said that, a long time ago, Timothy's great grandparents used to travel when they were young and they would pack all their stuff in those big trunks. He called them steamer trunks. He said that no one used them anymore. It was more fashionable now to have a set of luggage. It was also a heck of a lot easier for people to carry luggage around, instead of the big steamer trunks.

He said the house they were living in used to belong to Timothy's great grandparents and, after their family moved into the house, they just didn't have the heart to get rid of the trunks. They had been there under the stairway for years and years.

His dad said that it was the same way with the attic. All the stuff up there, the stuff that Timothy liked to explore through and play with, belonged to past family members and, over the years, it had just collected up in the attic. It was a good out-of-the-way storage area.

He said it was a central location in case anyone in the family, their aunts and uncles, decided that they wanted what he called 'family heirlooms' that were up there. He said that the stuff up there would most likely be there long after they were all gone.

Timothy knew all about the attic and what was stored up there. He always loved digging through the stuff that was stacked up and piled up all over the big room. He had gotten some of his very best ideas from up in the attic. He wasn't sure why he didn't find the attic spooky. Maybe, he thought, it was because it was warm up in the attic and it seemed chilly and moist down in the basement. He much preferred the attic.

But, being in the spooky basement with his dad gave him an excellent idea. It would be his very best joke ever. The great idea came to him while he was watching his dad and his mother came down to do the laundry.

The lightbulb went on in his head. His dad always said that, when you had a good idea, a lightbulb in your head lit up to let you know that the idea was a good one. Timothy had never seen the light go off in his head, but he was sure he had one because he'd had some really great ideas over the years.

This new joke would be awesome. He couldn't wait to tell his friend, Scotty, about his new idea. He shared the plan with Scotty and he agreed that it was *indeed* the best idea Timothy had ever had.

"Here's the plan," he explained to Scotty when they were in his room. "Since my sisters have to go down into the basement to do their laundry, I can look at the chart in the kitchen and find out when they are going to be down there. I'll get into one of those trunks and, when they come and open the trunk, I can jump out."

"How are you going to get them to open the trunk?" Scotty asked.

"Maybe I can knock on the trunk and they'll come over and open it," Timothy answered.

He set up his joke ahead of time. He put some blankets and a flashlight into one of the trunks under the stairs so he would be warm while he was waiting and he would have a light if he needed it.

He checked the chart in the kitchen. He saw that Tayla would be doing her laundry on Saturday around five o'clock. He was hoping for a great scream that would be even better than the scarecrow scream.

Saturday finally rolled around – and a storm rolled around with it. It was a pretty good storm too. By three o'clock in the afternoon it was really dark outside. He was a little concerned about the storm. The lightning and thunder worried him.

He wondered if he should postpone his joke for another day. Would Tayla even hear him knocking on the trunk with the thunder booming outside?

Also, the thought of being down in the spooky basement all alone waiting for Tayla to come down made him hesitate. He considered the situation and he decided to go ahead with the joke. Maybe the storm would make it even better when he jumped out of the trunk and surprised her.

At four o'clock, Timothy snuck down into the basement. He wanted to be set, just in case Tayla decided to start early. He knew from the chart that no one was scheduled to do laundry before her.

Timothy was cautious. The loud thunder outside made him nervous and the lightning that lit up the basement windows was scary. But, he reasoned, he would be in the trunk and he wouldn't see the lightning, and he would probably barely hear the thunder. Besides, he told himself, the lights were on in the basement. What was there to be nervous about?

He went down into the basement and he got into the trunk where he had put his stuff a few days before.

He kept the lid of the trunk open a crack for a few minutes so he could get used to the dark space. Then, he closed the lid and settled down to wait. It seemed like he was waiting a really long time. He wished he had brought a snack with him.

Timothy could barely hear the thunder. He looked at his watch and he could see that, what had seemed like a really long time had only been fifteen minutes. He wondered just how long this joke was going to take. Boy, time dragged slowly when you're waiting

Wait! He suddenly heard a sound – *knock, knock*. He froze in place. Maybe he *didn't* really hear anything, he told himself. After all, *he* was the one who was supposed to be knocking.

He sat still and listened. Then – *knock, knock*. It wasn't real loud, but he was sure he heard it. He was certain he hadn't imagined it. After only a minute, the tapping came again – *knock, knock.*

What if it came from inside the trunk with him? The thought alarmed him! Timothy groped around for the flashlight. When he located it, he snatched it up and turned it on. He quickly swept it back and forth so he could see around the inside of the trunk. He was relieved to see that he was alone.

Knock, knock. The tapping sounded nearby! Another thought occurred to him: what if it was coming from right outside of his trunk? It could be a ghost! Or, maybe a monster! If it was right outside of his trunk, then he was trapped!

Timothy was scared … almost too scared to think. Should he jump out of the trunk and try to run upstairs? If he jumped out would the monster be waiting to grab him? Would Tayla come down to do her laundry and scare the monster away? He was afraid to make a decision.

Knock, knock. The knocking was making his heart beat faster. Then he heard another sound. Was that moaning, he wondered? Woo-o-o-o! Woo-o-o-o! His fast-beating heart almost stopped! It wasn't a whistle sound, like the wind would make. It sounded deep. It was low and slow – like someone, or something would make … something like a monster would make! A MONSTER! He had seen the movies about people-eating monsters! He was petrified at the thought a monster was prowling around the trunk, waiting for him to come out! It would run after him, snarling and slobbering, and pounce on him, just like he had seen in the movies!

Knock, knock. The tapping came again, followed by the low moan. He became terrified. He had to get away! He had to make a run for it! Don't get trapped in this trunk, he shouted inside his head! He was trembling with fear. He had to decide what to do. He tried to swallow but his throat was too dry.

Okay, he said to himself, do you sit here and let the monster get you, or do you fight your way out like in the video games? You have to try and get away, he answered himself. Scotty would be proud of him – that is, if he lived to tell him about it. He decided that he would make a break for it. It was the only way ... his only chance for survival!

He braced himself. He hoped he wouldn't die of fright when he saw the monster. He decided that he would keep his head down. When he felt ready, he closed his eyes, pushed open the lid, and quickly jumped out of the trunk. He turned to run for the stairs but he stopped abruptly! Timothy thought his heart stopped too at the shock! Wait!

Two of his sisters were standing in the middle of the room looking at him. Tami had her arms folded across her chest and Tayla had her hands on her hips. They both had smirky smiles on their faces.

"Well, what's going on here, Little Uh-oh?" Tami asked.

"Yeah," Tayla added, "what's happening down here? Just what are you up to?"

Timothy was so relieved to see his sisters that he thought he might cry. He was so glad there was no monster lurking around waiting for him.

Suddenly, the lid of the other trunk burst open and Teddi jumped up. "BOO!" she yelled loudly.

Timothy was caught off guard. He had relaxed at the sight of his sisters. Now, his body stiffened with fright. He jumped and fell onto the floor in fear. He curled up in a ball with his arms over his head – and he screamed! It was a really loud scream!

After a few moments, Timothy realized he wasn't in any danger. He uncovered his head and looked up.

Teddi said, "You know what happened? I heard you explaining your *'great new joke'* to Scotty and I had my own idea for a great new joke."

"Yeah," Tayla chimed in, "best scream EVER!"

The End

It was a dark and stormy night ...

Vivian and Grace

Vivian was in the kitchen with Grace, her good friend from school. They were trying to bake some cookies. They weren't quite sure what they were doing, but they were determined to make ten dozen cookies for a bake sale.

They had never actually baked before, not without being supervised. But, they decided, because they were now in high school, they were sure they could figure it out.

"How hard can it be?" Vivian had asked.

Grace had just shrugged her shoulders and the decision was made – they would be baking cookies.

One of their classmates had a car accident and he was in the hospital. Vivian and Grace had the idea to host a fundraiser to raise money to help the student pay his hospital bills. They organized a bake sale to be held at school. The sale was the next day and they had waited until the last minute to bake the cookies so they would be super fresh.

The school principal gave his blessing to the idea and the two girls got busy arranging for the bake sale. A couple of boys who were on the yearbook staff created some really cool posters and they printed some flyers. They hung up the posters around the school and the flyers were posted around the area in store windows and on telephone poles. The flyers explained the reason for the fundraiser and asked people to drop by the school and purchase cookies and other baked goods to help with a good cause.

From what Vivian and Grace had heard about the feedback from the advertising, they were expecting a big turnout for the event. They asked for volunteers to make baked goods and a number of students signed up to help. Some of them volunteered their mothers to do the baking.

From all the things listed on the sign-up sheet, it looked like the sale would have a nice variety of items to help the fundraiser be a big success. There would be plenty of yummy things for sale. Vivian and Grace were excited. They were glad they had the idea.

Many students and even some of the teachers had been congratulating them and thanking them all day for their hard work in organizing the event.

Vivian and Grace knew that the other volunteers were busy in their homes baking like crazy for the sale. The girls were a little disappointed when it started raining the night before. A storm had moved into the area and it had lingered all day. There was some thunder, and a lot of rain, but there wasn't very much lightning. They talked about the weather and realized that it wouldn't affect the bake sale. It would be held inside the school, so the weather didn't matter. That idea cheered them right up.

Grace came over to Vivian's house right after dinner so they could get started. It was already dark when she got there. The rain had stopped, but they could still hear the thunder. The dark clouds were still filling up the whole sky, so they expected that the clouds weren't finished dumping rain on the area. The weather forecast said to expect more rain throughout the following day.

Since they were unsure of just how to get started, they agreed that they had to get organized. Grace suggested they get out everything they would need so they wouldn't forget anything. Vivian agreed that it was an excellent idea and said that she should have thought of it herself. The girls laughed at that.

As Grace read the ingredients from the recipe, Vivian gathered the items and put them on the counter. Since it was her house, they decided it would be best if she did the gathering because she knew exactly where everything was stored.

After all the ingredients were lined up on the counter, Vivian took out measuring cups and some containers. Grace read the amounts the recipe asked for and Vivian measured them out perfectly and put them into separate containers. Then, Vivian got out cookie sheets. She lined them with some parchment paper that her mother had showed her how to use.

Once they felt organized, and were sure they had everything assembled, they felt more confident about tackling their project.

Vivian turned on the oven. Grace started to read the order in which the ingredients should be added to the mixing bowl Vivian was using to make the cookie dough.

Vivian added the items and stirred the dough as Grace read them to her.

Suddenly, Grace stopped in the middle of the sentence she was reading. "Wait!" "Did you hear anything?" she asked, looking up at Vivian.

"I wasn't paying attention," Vivian answered.

"I thought I heard something," Grace explained.

"I was only listening to you," Vivian said. "What did you hear?"

"I'm not sure. It sounded like someone talking," Grace replied. "It was kind of low, but it sounded like voices nearby."

"There's no one home," Vivian said. "We're the only ones here. There shouldn't be anybody talking."

"H-m-m-m, maybe I imagined it," Grace wondered aloud. "It *was* kind of faint."

"Maybe it was the thunder," Vivian suggested. "Sometimes noise like that can sound like talking or music or something. I think I read somewhere that your brain tries to sort out stuff to understand it."

They went back to mixing their cookie dough.

After a few minutes Grace stopped again. "Wait! Are you sure you don't hear anything?" she asked. "I'm sure I hear someone talking."

Vivian paused and listened. "Hey," she exclaimed, "you're right. I think I hear someone talking too."

"Maybe it's somebody outside," Grace suggested.

"I don't think anyone should be out there," Vivian said, shaking her head. "Do you mean in the backyard?"

"Uh, I don't know," Grace said, "just outside somewhere. What about out in the driveway? Maybe some of your neighbors are out there talking to each other."

"Well, we've almost got all of the stuff in here to make the cookie dough," Vivian said, nodding toward the bowl where she had been stirring like crazy. "Let's get the rest of those things in here and we'll check it out before we start baking.

"Okay," Grace answered. She read the last of the ingredients and Vivian added them to the bowl. She blended all of the items together with a big spoon and created the dough.

"Okay, that's finished," she finally said. "I think we're ready for the next step, which is the cooking part."

"Good," Grace said, "so far, so good, right? Let's make sure we haven't forgotten anything up to this point."

"You're right," Vivian agreed. "Once we cook them it'll be too late if we overlooked something."

As they were going back over the recipe steps and verifying the amounts of each ingredient they had added, they both heard muffled sounds.

"See," said Grace, "somebody is talking outside."

Vivian went to the kitchen window and looked out. "There's no one in the backyard," she said.

"What about the driveway?" Grace asked.

Vivian went into the living room and opened the front door. She didn't believe that someone would be out in the storm talking in the driveway. Maybe, she thought, something has happened, like a tree limb falling or something, and the neighbors are out there talking about it.

She stepped out onto the porch. She went to either side of the porch and looked around. As she was looking, a flash of lightning lit up the area. She could clearly see the length of the driveway in the lightning flash. There wasn't anyone there, not in her driveway, nor the neighbor's driveway on the opposite side of the house.

She went back to the kitchen where Grace was waiting. "There's no one out there anywhere," she told her friend.

"While you were gone, I thought I heard it again," Grace said. "It was right after that thunder."

"Maybe it *is* the thunder," Vivian said. "It could be an echo of the thunder. That could be it."

Grace tilted her head and listened. "No, I don't think it's an echo," she said. "There's no thunder now and I think I can still hear them talking."

Vivian listened too. "Oh, that's spooky," she said. "I can hear it too. Where's it coming from?"

"I think it's behind us," said Grace.

The girls turned and looked behind them as if they thought they would see some people standing there talking. They heard muffled talking.

"I think it's definitely back here somewhere and not up at the front of the house," Vivian said.

"You're right, it's somewhere back here," Grace agreed. "What's back here?"

"Nothing," Vivian said, looking around. "There's the kitchen and the pantry." She went over to the food closet that her mother called a pantry and she opened the door.

It was just a small room lined with shelves for storing canned goods and other things that didn't go into the refrigerator. The room was empty. "Nothing there," she said, as she returned to Grace.

"There's got to be something else," Grace said. "It's back here somewhere. I can hear it. Could it be upstairs?"

"I don't think so," Vivian answered. "My brother's room is over the kitchen and he's not there. He left yesterday to go to our uncle's house to help him paint his house. He'll be gone for a week. So, it can't be coming from up there."

"Well, then, what's that other door?" Grace asked, pointing to a door on the other side of the pantry.

"That's the door to the basement," Vivian replied.

The girls stopped and looked at each other as the idea was forming. Their eyes widened as they realized that the basement was the only place left that they hadn't thought of. They stood perfectly still, staring at each other, and they listened closely.

Then they heard it – muffled voices. They realized that the voices were coming from the basement! They watched each other's face as they grasped the truth. They read the fear in each other's eyes and they froze.

"Someone's down there!" Grace whispered. She sounded scared. "What should we do?"

"I hear that," Vivian said. She was feeling afraid too. "What are they doing down there? How did they get down there?"

"Maybe it's your mom and dad," Grace suggested.

"No, they're gone," Vivian responded. "They went to a birthday party at someone's house. If my mom was home, she'd be helping us make these cookies. No, it's definitely not them down there."

"Wow," Grace breathed loudly, "then someone's in your basement. Do you have any ghosts?"

"No, we don't have ghosts," Vivian said.

"Then, there are strangers in your house!" Grace exclaimed "They're probably robbers. Let's get out of here!"

"No, wait," Vivian said. "Let's make sure."

"What ... are you out of your mind?" Grace asked in disbelief.

"No, wait here," Vivian said. "I'll go check."

"I'm not waiting here alone," Grace said.

They crept over to the basement. Vivian slowly turned the knob. She very quietly opened the door so as not to make a sound. She only opened the door a small crack. The two girls leaned close to the opening and listened intently. They could hear muffled voices.

They turned their faces toward each other. The terror on Vivian's face mirrored the terror on Grace's face. The girls were terrified and they stood staring at each other until Grace finally blinked.

Vivian softly closed the door and the girls backed away.

Grace said, "See, I told you. There are robbers in your house! Now, can we get out of here?" She nodded her head in a gesture that they should go.

Vivian shook her head in agreement. Without another word, the girls turned at the same time and raced for the front door.

As they reached the door, Grace jerked open the door and terrified Vivian ran out, followed closely by terrified Grace.

Vivian's parents were coming up the front porch steps and she ran right into her father's arms. Vivian was surprised that her parents were right there and she almost fainted from the shock.

"Good gracious!" her mother exclaimed.

'Wow, where are you girls headed to?" her father asked. "Is the house on fire?"

"There are robbers in the house!" Vivian gasped.

"Robbers?" her father asked. He looked confused.

"Yeah," Grace added, "we heard them talking in the basement. They scared the life out of us."

"Let me go and have a look," her father said.

"Be careful, Charles," Vivian's mother said.

He just nodded his head. With a determined look on his face he went into the house. Vivian went down the steps with her mother and stood on the sidewalk in front of the porch. Grace went and stood next to Vivian. After just a few minutes, Vivian's father came out through the front door.

"Did you catch them?" her mother asked.

'Where are they?" Vivian asked. "Are they down there?"

"Vivian," her father said, "did you two go down into the basement?"

"No, we were too scared," Vivian answered. "We just opened the door and closed it."

"Well, there's nothing to be afraid of," he said, looking at Vivian. "I was working in the basement earlier today. You know that when I'm down there I listen to talk radio. I forgot and I left the radio on, that's all. It's nothing more exciting than that. I would have thought you'd realize what the sound was when you heard it."

"I think we were too scared by then," Vivian said.

"Terrified, you mean," Grace added.

"Yeah, Dad," Vivian said. "We weren't about to go down there and look around."

"Well, if you two didn't go down there I can understand that you may not have realized what was going on, especially if you were scared. When you're scared and your imagination starts running, there's no telling where you could end up."

He smiled. "I apologize to you girls. I didn't mean to frighten you," he said.

"All's well, then," Vivian's mother said. "Come on you girls, let's go bake some cookies."

The End

It was a dark and stormy night ...

Wait! ... What?

Eleven-year-old Brayden had a vivid imagination. Everyone knew it, especially his family. He made up fantastic stories from his imagination and he loved to act them out for his family.

He had two older brothers, Grant and Tristan, and even though they were teenagers, they patiently listened to all of his fanciful tales. They were always amused by his dramatic telling of his stories.

He had one younger sister. Her name was Violet. She absolutely loved his stories. Violet was Brayden's very favorite audience. He created special stories for her, wonderful stories that included all of her favorite stuffed animals from her bedroom.

Although everyone else called him Brayden, his father called him Bee-boy. He encouraged Brayden to write down his tales and keep them in a special folder so he could go back and read them again and again. There was also the possibility that Brayden could create a book from his great stories.

They lived in a town where there was a college. Brayden's father was an English professor there. He said the college had a publishing department that he called the *College Press*. He told Brayden that, if he could put together all of his stories, he might be able to persuade them to publish his book for him.

Brayden was intrigued by the idea that he could create a book and share his most awesome stories with anyone in the world who wanted to read them. He was anxious to get started on the project.

Tristan, who was really good at drawing stuff, told him that, if he wrote enough good stories to make a book, he would draw some pictures for the stories and also create a cover for the book.

Brayden was really delighted at the prospect of making his very own book and he set about writing down the stories in a notebook. He didn't think his spelling was so good, but he decided that the spelling could be fixed later. He felt that getting the idea of the story down on paper was the most important thing – before he forgot the story completely. Grant told him that he would correct all the spelling for him whenever he got finished with all the stories and it was ready to be looked at.

While he was writing the stories, he also got new ideas for even more stories. He had a special 'ideas' section in the back of the notebook where he would write down those new ideas.

His bedtime was around eight o'clock. His parents insisted that it was *lights out* at that time. But, when he was in the middle of a really good story, he felt he just *had* to finish it. It was important. Heck, he said to himself, by morning he may not remember all the good details and he'd have to start all over in the story to make it turn out right.

There was a small apartment complex next door to Brayden's house where college students could rent apartments. The complex had sidewalks that were lighted at night and one of the sidewalks went right past his window. Brayden thought that it was perfect, that it was *meant to be* ... it was destiny! He could use the light from the walkways to see after it was *lights out* at his house.

At night, he would open up the curtains in his room and the light from the walkway would shine right onto his bed. He had plenty of light to finish writing a story that he was in the middle of – it was great – so perfect!

One night, when there was a storm, he had a story that was almost finished and he was eager to get to the end of it. Brayden had thought of a really great ending where there was a surprise and he was worried that he would forget if he didn't finish it right away.

He put his writing notebook under the cover so his mother wouldn't see it when she looked in on him before she went to bed. He waited and it didn't seem too long before he heard his parents getting ready for bed. Brayden knew his father had a class that he had to teach early in the mornings, so they never stayed up very late.

He got up and opened the curtains right after his mother peeked into his room and closed the door. He knew that she wouldn't come back. Even when there was a storm, the lights along the sidewalk outside his window were always on.

He decided that the storm must be moving away because he could barely hear the thunder, rumbling across the sky in the distance. The rain had stopped too.

Some of the lightning was still around, but it wasn't very bright, so he knew that it was also moving away.

He got out the notebook and opened it on his bed. While he was trying to remember what came next in the story, he saw a shadow passing his window. He looked up and saw that it was just two of the students who lived in the apartment complex walking by. He was used to seeing the students go past. They didn't seem to keep the early hours that his parents did. They always seemed to be up late.

Brayden wasn't sure why, but whenever someone walked by, he always looked up. He thought that it was a curious thing to do because he already knew who was going by. But he just couldn't help it. He looked anyway, like it was automatic or something.

After a couple of shadows went past, and he looked up to see the students walking by, he would go back to his writing. When he looked up at the same time that the lightning flashed, it was hard to see exactly who it was walking along. By now, he was familiar with most of the students – they walked by every day and most of them had been living over there for a while.

Brayden was writing along, coming to a good part of his story, when a shadow started past his window. He glanced up just as the lightning flashed.

The lightning kind of blinded him for a second but he froze. Wait! What? A monster was walking down the sidewalk!

He was instantly frightened. In only a moment the monster was gone. He wasn't quite sure he had really seen it. After all, why would a monster be walking down the sidewalk? He thought about that and it sounded reasonable to him – he just didn't see it correctly. He imagined it. The lightning had blinded him and he mistook one of the students for something else. That's all it was, he assured himself. He had just jumped to a conclusion, as his father was always saying.

Brayden scolded himself for being so silly. He shrugged off the idea and returned to his writing. After a few minutes, he noticed a shadow passing the other way and he took a quick look. Again, the lightning flashed and again he saw the monster! He suddenly realized what it was! It was the lagoon creature he had seen on television!

He was sure he wasn't imagining it and he knew the lightning didn't blind him enough that he couldn't see clearly. That lagoon creature was outside his house! He had seen it twice!

He felt the prickly fear swarming over his body and making the little hairs on his arms stand up. Brayden slid off the side of the bed and backed over to his bedroom door. He groped behind him until he found the door knob. He quietly opened the door and slipped out into the hall.

Brayden went down the hall to his parents room, opened their door, and creeped inside. His parents were sound asleep. He went over to his father's side of the bed. He shook his father gently.

"Dad," he whispered as he was shaking his father, "Dad!"

"What is it there, Bee-boy?" his father answered sleepily.

He wasn't waking up.

"Dad, there's a monster outside my room," Brayden whispered close to his father's ear.

"What kind of monster?" his father asked groggily.

"It's the lagoon creature that I saw on television," Brayden explained.

"What were you doing watching that kind of movie?" his father asked.

"I watched it with Grant and Tristan," Brayden said.

"They're not supposed to be letting you see those movies," his father said.

"But, the lagoon monster is outside my room, Dad," Brayden explained.

"You just tell it to go away or it'll end up in one of your stories, Bee-boy," his father said.

Brayden could tell his father wasn't taking it seriously and he wasn't going to wake up. Suddenly, he thought of Grant. Grant would help him.

Brayden slipped out of his parents' room and silently closed the door. Grant and Tristan had their bedrooms on the second floor. He'd have to go upstairs. He felt he would have to hurry before the creature got into the house. He ran down to the stairway and he went up the steps.

He went to Grant's room, tapped on the door, and opened it. Grant was sitting at his desk over by the window.

"What do you want?" Grant asked, looking up from his laptop.

"Grant," Brayden said breathlessly. He was out of breath from racing up the stairs. "There's a monster outside!"

"Nonsense," Grant answered.

"No, for real and for true," Brayden said. "There's a monster walking around outside!"

"There's no monster," Grant assured him.

"Sure there is," Brayden said.

"No," Grant said, "there's no monster. Do you want me to tell you what it is?"

"I know what it is," Brayden responded, "It's the lagoon creature from the movie!"

Grant just laughed. Brayden was confused. He wondered if Grant had lost his mind. The lagoon monster was outside and he was laughing? That didn't figure.

"I've been sitting here for a while," Grant said. "I know what you saw outside there on the sidewalk. I saw it too."

"Oh, good, then you saw the monster," Brayden interrupted.

"No," Grant went on, "it wasn't a monster. Well, it *was* a monster, but it wasn't real."

"HUH?" Brayden said back. Now he really was convinced that Grant had lost his marbles.

"Come over here and look," Grant directed.

Brayden went across the room and stood next to his brother.

Grant pointed out the window, to an apartment across the way. "Look over there," he said.

Brayden followed Grant's pointing finger. He looked across at the apartment complex and he saw the creature in the living room of one of the apartments! He drew back in shock!

"It's in somebody's apartment," Brayden said in panic. "It got in there!"

"Look closer," Grant said. "It's a statue."

"What?" Brayden exclaimed. "It was walking! I saw it walking down the sidewalk! It walked right past my window!"

"No, it was being carried," Grant said. "I saw the dude who was carrying it. He went past to show it to his buddies in that apartment over there." He pointed to the rear building. "Then, he came back and took it up to his apartment."

"A statue," Brayden said in wonder. "I thought it was walking." He could plainly see that it really was a statue. It was standing there in the living room of the guy who lived across the way.

Grant said, "It was being carried. It was bouncing up and down because that dude was carrying it. If it was walking, it would have been moving smoother."

"No way," Brayden said.

"Think about it," Grant said.

"There was lightning," Brayden said, "it looked just like it was walking."

"Maybe I had a better view from up here," Grant said. "I was looking down on it so I probably got a better look than you did."

"Yeah," Brayden agreed. "Boy, am I glad?" And he really was.

Grant smiled. "It's that imagination of yours," he said. "You never know where it's going to take you."

"Yeah," Brayden said, sighing with relief.

"Well, now you have a new idea for a story," Grant said.

The End

X-travaganza!

Harrison Huntsmerritt was ten years old and he loved magic. He had been fascinated by it ever since he saw a magic show on television way back when he was like seven years old.

He had many books about magic and he had practiced the tricks over and over again. He spent all of his allowance on 'magic supplies' and he even did odd jobs around the neighborhood to get more money for the things he would need for his magic act.

He had a little folding table that he could set up for his act. His dad had found the table stored in the attic and he thought it would work for Harrison's act. It was perfect. His mom made him a cover for the table. It was black cloth with gold stars and yellow moons on it. It was perfect too. He had made a sign to hang on the front of his magic table that read *Harrison Huntsmerritt: Expert Magician.* He looked at his display and he was *not* impressed. The name was all wrong.

He spent several days looking at the sign hanging from the front edge of the table. Nope, that just won't do, he said to himself. It was the name. It just wasn't special enough. He thought and thought but he could not come up with any ideas for anything different. He needed something that would stand out – something that made him sound awesome and fantastic.

He asked his dad for an idea. "Well, Little H," he said, "it should be something that has a *'ring'* to it, something *'catchy'* that people will remember." His dad had always called him Little H. He had gotten used to it over the years. His dad suggested that Harrison should sleep on it. He said that the best ideas come while you are asleep.

So, before he went to sleep that night, Harrison reminded himself to think of an idea while he was sleeping. In the morning, he decided that his dad was right because, when he woke up, he had a great idea.

He had read about a very famous magician in one of his books. He got right out of bed and tracked down the book on one of his shelves. He made a decision. He was very excited about the new name for his act. It was such a great idea that he could hardly wait to tell his dad.

The minute he got out of bed, even before breakfast, he immediately made a new sign. It read: *Harrison Houdini: Master Magician's X-travaganza!*

He hung the new sign on the front of his magician's table. He stood back to admire it. It was so perfect. It was so excellent!

With his hands on his hips, he declared out loud, "That's it!" As he read his new sign, he announced to his room, "From this very day, and from now on, until forever, my act will be known as *Harrison Houdini: Master Magician's X-travaganza!*"

He was delighted! He raced downstairs to tell his parents. All through breakfast he went on and on about the awesome idea and how he dreamed it up in his sleep. He was so proud. Both of his parents agreed that the name was perfect for him. The fact that the first name of the famous magician was *Harry* was not lost on them.

He set up his magician's table in the living room and made his brothers, Chase and Mason, watch him perform his act again and again. They watched him present his X-travaganza magic act tricks so many times that they started to believe they could probably do them too.

After a couple of weeks they had seen the act so many times that, when Harrison Houdini wanted them to watch again, they *suddenly* remembered that they had something else they *had* to do immediately.

Every night, before Harrison went to bed, he made sure all of his magic stuff was put away. He put his tablecloth in a drawer, folded up his table, and arranged his magic tricks on the dresser across the room.

On Saturday afternoon, he put on his act at a place where his mom worked taking care of people's grandfathers and grandmothers. His mom said one of the grandmothers was having her 86th birthday party and she thought it would be a lot of fun for the people there to see his magic act.

Harrison wore his top hat, his long cape, and his special white gloves. He had a great time and his audience clapped and clapped. His mother said they loved the act. She said that Harrison had made it a really special occasion. He was very pleased with the praise. After he finished his act, his dad took his magic stuff home and

Harrison stayed behind to help his mom serve cake and ice cream to the residents at the party.

When he got home his dad told him that Chase and Mason had put his things away for him. He stayed downstairs until bedtime watching television. He was a little tired from the excitement of putting on his magic act for a big audience. It had been a really good day. He was ready for sleep when he finally went up to his room.

Harrison fell into bed and he was asleep within a few minutes. In his sleep, he could hear rumbling. It didn't bother him enough to wake him up at first. But, after a while, it got louder and then a really big boom of thunder shook the windows in his room. He jerked awake in surprise! He could see lightning flashing outside his window.

Harrison could see that Mason's light was on in his room across the hall. His brothers were teenagers and they always stayed up later than he did.

He sat up and turned on the lamp beside his bed. He didn't care much for thunder storms and the lightning was scary when it was really bright. Thunder storms always made it hard for him to sleep because he was afraid of the lightning and they made him feel anxious. He could see the rain tapping against the window.

Wait! Suddenly, from the corner of his eye, he saw a movement. He turned his head quickly to see what it was. One of the handkerchiefs that he used in his act was lifting off the dresser! He was shocked! The handkerchief floated straight up, halfway to the ceiling and then it floated back down to the dresser. He was puzzled. He wondered – what the heck?

As he watched, the handkerchief lifted up again and floated back down again. He was bewildered. How could that happen, he wondered? Then the handkerchief did it again!

It was spooky. While he was trying to decide whether it was something to be scared of, there was a little movement beside the handkerchief. He looked at his deck of magic cards on the dresser. The top card lifted up from the deck and floated up into the air!

Harrison felt the chill bumps running all over his body. Then, a second card floated up into the air! Then a third card floated up! He was instantly terrified! Then the handkerchief floated up again!

Wait! It was a GHOST! Harrison realized that there was a ghost in his room! He decided that it had to be a ghost. What else could it be? He was very frightened.

He jumped out of bed and raced out of the room. He ran to his parents' room but they weren't there. He turned and ran down the stairs.

"Dad!" he yelled as he ran into the living room.

"Hey, Little H," his dad exclaimed, "what's the matter? Are you okay?"

"No, Dad, there's a ghost in my room," Harrison blurted out. "We have a ghost in the house!"

"No, no, that's not possible," his dad said.

"Yeah, Dad," Harrison explained, "stuff is floating all around my room! There's a ghost moving stuff all over the place in there."

His dad stood up. "Let's go have a look," he said. He glanced at Harrison's mom and she smiled.

"C'mon," Harrison answered. "I'll show you."

"Let's just go check this out," his dad said.

He followed his dad up the stairs and down the hall to his room. They stopped in the doorway. Everything in the room looked normal.

"Okay," his dad said, "what am I looking at?"

"I don't get it," Harrison answered. "There was stuff floating around."

"What stuff? Which things were floating?" his dad asked.

"That cloth over there on the dresser," Harrison said, pointing at the handkerchief. "And those cards were floating around too."

His dad went over to the dresser to get a closer look. After only a moment he turned back toward Harrison. He held out his hands and hanging from one hand was a card and from the other hand was the handkerchief. They were swinging back and forth.

Harrison asked, "What is it?"

"Strings," his dad said. "They're all attached to strings." He looked up at the ceiling. "The strings are running through those little hooks up on the ceiling."

"What does it mean, Dad?" Harrison asked.

"I'll tell you exactly what it means," his dad said. He looked toward the door and he yelled. "Mason! Chase! You two get in here right now!"

His brothers came out of their rooms and came into Harrison's room.

Before either one of them could speak, their dad said, "Okay, you two, let's have it."

"What?" Chase was trying to sound innocent.

"You know exactly what I'm talking about," their dad said, holding up the items dangling from the strings in his hands.

Both of his brothers busted out laughing.

"Now, that's enough," their dad said, holding up his hands with the cloth and the cards swinging from them. "Let's have that explanation."

The brothers stopped laughing and Mason spoke. "Darn it! We spent two hours yesterday setting up those tricks. And we didn't even get to show all of them."

"Go on," their dad said, "tell your brother what's going on here so he's knows there's no ghost."

"Well," Chase said, "he made us watch his magic show so many times that we thought maybe we would just show him some magic of our own."

"Yeah," Mason said, "we rigged up those strings and we hid behind the drapes after he went to sleep. When he woke up we just pulled the strings to make the stuff move around. We were just joking."

"It was really cool," Chase chimed in.

"No, not so cool," their dad answered. "As you can see, Little H here didn't get the joke. It's always funny until somebody gets scared. Now, you two will come in here tomorrow and remove all the contraptions you set up to play your joke."

"Okay," Mason said.

"All right," Chase added. "Sorry about that little man. We won't do that to you again."

"Okay," Harrison said, accepting the apology.

"Then, after you clear out your magic tricks, you can take Little H out for ice cream," their dad said.

"Hooray!" Harrison shouted.

The End

It was a dark and stormy night ...

Yvonne

Yvonne was babysitting. It was something that she loved to do. She had been caring for people's children since she was thirteen years old. Her sister used to babysit for some of the neighbors and, when her sister left for college, Yvonne stepped in and took over watching the children for those families.

It wasn't very long before her customers began to recommend her to other neighbors and, later on, to their friends who lived outside the neighborhood. By the time she started driving, she was babysitting for families all over town.

Yvonne was crazy about children. She enjoyed interacting with them so much that she decided to become an elementary school teacher. She felt that being a teacher would make her really happy and she was looking forward to spending her career teaching children. When she graduated high school and left for college, she was excited about getting her teaching degree and coming back home to teach.

Soon after she arrived at college, she saw a notice on the bulletin board that the students used to communicate with each other. The notice was asking for students to apply and join a group of other students who worked as babysitters for extra money.

Yvonne asked around and learned that, several years before, a group of students at the college created a service so that they could earn money by babysitting and housesitting around the town. As the older members graduated and left the college, newer students would join the group and take their places. So, the service continued from year to year with some students leaving and new students joining and they were successful. The group put up notices around town and they also advertised in the local newspaper and on the college radio station. The families they worked for also told other families about them and they were always getting new customers.

The service was run like a regular business. They had their business license and all the members were bonded – Yvonne found out that it meant they were insured. Knowing that the students watching their children and their homes were bonded made their customers feel better about hiring them.

The group of students who originally created the service called it *Sitting Ink*. The 'sitting' part was for the service they offered and the 'ink' part was for the contracts that they signed with the customers. The contracts explained all the details of the service, what the students promised to do, and the prices they set for the work.

Yvonne really liked the idea of the sitting service. She gave them her references so she could join the company. After the active members called the families she worked for back in her home town, they eagerly welcomed her into the group.

Yvonne had been working with them for several months. She had watched children a bunch of times and she stayed over in homes three times while families were out of town. There always seemed to be work available for the group. They were very popular with the people in the town.

The families that she was sitting for began to request her, which really delighted her. She loved babysitting because, as a student, she could always find the time to spend on her schoolwork after the children went to sleep or while families were out of town and the house was quiet.

Yvonne was babysitting for a new customer the service had just signed a contract with. The Martin family had three children who were all under ten years old. The parents rushed off soon after she arrived. They were invited to attend a special dinner with Mr. Martin's employer and, because there was a storm, they wanted to get an early start to ensure they got there on time.

Yvonne fed the children the dinner that Mrs. Martin had already prepared. After dinner, she played games with the children, and they spent some time coloring in the kids' coloring books. She really liked that. She had colored with lots of children over the years. It helped her feel creative. She loved to show them how to pay close attention so that they colored inside the lines. She showed them how to match colors so that their pictures would be special.

Working with them was so much fun for her and she made sure it was fun for them too. She even brought coloring books and crayons with her to every babysitting job. It made her feel like she was already a teacher. She knew that she was sitting with children who were around the ages she would be teaching after she graduated.

The kids had been a little restless because of the storm outside. They weren't exactly afraid, but they seemed nervous. She talked to them about being brave and how to ignore the storm, because it was outside. She explained that they were safe indoors where nothing could harm them and they seemed satisfied with that.

It was something that *her* father had taught her. And she had 'weathered' many a storm, as he would say – then he would laugh at the joke he made about the storm and the weather. He said it was called a 'pun' and that it was a joke because of the way the two words were put together – the storm *was* the weather. He was right ... she had been safe through every storm. As a child, it helped her to not be afraid and to have confidence.

Once the storm started moving away, the children relaxed and, after a while, they became sleepy. She read them a story and put them to bed. She had let them stay up a little longer than they were supposed to because of the storm.

Even though the storm passed, the wind was still blowing. She could hear it. She decided that the wind had blown the storm away. She was fine with that.

After a while, the house was quiet. Yvonne checked on the children and they were all asleep. She settled down on the floor in front of the coffee table and leaned back against the sofa. She took books from her backpack and got ready to study. Her semester finals were in a week and she wanted to get an early start studying for the exams. She was taking five classes and she wanted to be sure she was ready for all of them.

She decided to start with the first class where she would have a test. She had just opened her book and started reading when she heard a sound. It was something like a soft, creaking sound. It wasn't very loud. She stopped reading and listened. In a few minutes she heard it again ... *Creak*! She wondered if one of the children had woken up.

She put her book down and stood up. She paused to listen, but she didn't hear anything. She went upstairs and checked on the children. They were all still asleep. She stood in the hall and listened for a few minutes. When she was satisfied that the sound wasn't upstairs and wasn't the children, she went back to the living room and sat down. She picked up her textbook and started to read.

After a minute or two, she heard the sound again. *Creak*! It wasn't really loud, but she thought it came from the rear of the house. She knew the back door was in a little entryway at the rear of the house. She had noticed it while she was in the kitchen getting dinner for the children.

She listened for a moment and she heard it. *Creak*! It was followed by something that sounded like a door being softly closed.

She got up and went into the kitchen. She could see that the back door was shut. She looked around. There weren't any other doors back there except the door to the basement. She went over to it and pushed on it. It was firmly closed. She went to the back door and pushed on it. It was also firmly closed. Then she checked the kitchen cabinets. They were all closed too. She couldn't figure out how any of the doors or cabinets could have made the sound.

Satisfied that all was well in the rear of the house, she turned and started out of the room. As she neared the door to the living room, she heard a sound behind her. *Creak!* She froze in place! She turned around and looked at the back door. It was slightly open. Wait! Hadn't she just checked that door?

Then, as she watched, the door closed itself. She wondered if maybe the door hadn't been properly closed, and perhaps the wind had blown it open. She went over and pushed on the door. She pushed on it harder than she had the first time. It seemed snugly in place. She turned the bolt on the door to lock it.

She turned to leave, but before she reached the doorway to the living room, she heard it. *Creak!*

She turned around and, sure enough, the door was open again. She was puzzled. She *knew* she had just locked it. She went over to the door. As she reached out her hand, the door closed on its own.

She drew back her hand in surprise. She took a few steps backwards and watched the door. After a minute the door opened a little again and made the creaking sound. *Creak!* She went over and opened the door. She looked out at the backyard. She didn't see anyone or anything else out of the ordinary.

It was curious. She listened for the wind that sounded strong earlier. It didn't seem to be blowing as hard now. She couldn't feel a draft either. She shook her head. If there wasn't any wind, how could the door open and close by itself? She took another look around and closed the door.

She pushed the door firmly closed and locked it. She stepped back and listened for the wind but she still couldn't hear it. She backed up toward the door to the living room, but she kept her eyes on the door. Just as she reached the doorway, the back door creaked open slightly. *Creak*!

Yvonne was spooked. It just wasn't making sense. If it wasn't the wind, then whatever could it be? She couldn't figure it out. Then, as she watched the door, it closed itself. She was suddenly afraid.

"Oh, no," Yvonne said out loud, "it's a ghost." She decided that it *had* to be a ghost. What else could open and close the door? It was really spooky. It was a ghost and it was trying to scare her ... and it was certainly working! She stood in the doorway.

The door opened and closed again. *Creak*! She was frightened. The family hadn't said anything about the house being haunted. She decided that if the house really was haunted, then she was super positive she didn't want to see a ghost. This was bad enough. Seeing the ghost would send her screaming out the front door. She was scared just from the door opening and closing. She didn't think she could handle seeing any kind of ghost.

She noticed that the ghost had waited until the children went asleep before it showed up. It must be trying to scare only her. When the door opened and closed again, she fought back a scream. She backed into the living room. She didn't want to turn her back on the ghost.

She wasn't sure of what she should do. Her father definitely had not prepared her for anything like this. She couldn't be brave in the face of something that was invisible and she surely couldn't be brave if she saw the ghost.

She was starting to feel terror creeping over her and making her feel itchy. She backed over to the coffee table. She gathered her books and put them in her backpack. She knew she wasn't going to be able to study with a ghost opening and closing the door. What if it followed her into the living room? What should she do? She couldn't leave the children. Should she go upstairs to protect them? Would the ghost try to harm them?

She was confused. She was having some trouble deciding what she should do. She wondered if she should wake up the children and get them out of the house. She knew that *she* would feel safer outside.

Yvonne picked up her backpack and she backed across the living room toward the front door. She kept her eyes glued on the doorway to the kitchen. She didn't see anything and she was so glad. *Creak*! She could still hear the door opening and closing every few minutes.

She backed into the entryway. As she got near the foot of the stairway which led upstairs, she put her backpack down on the floor at the foot of the steps.

She was preparing to back up the stairs when the front door suddenly swung open. She jumped back in fright and a little squeal escaped from her mouth. She stumbled against the first step and she fell backwards onto the stairs. She was really terrified! She was wide-eyed and she was panting because she couldn't catch her breath.

Mr. and Mrs. Martin rushed forward together into the entryway.

"What happened, Yvonne," Mrs. Martin asked, and she seemed to be out of breath too. Her eyes were also opened wide and she looked frightened. "What's the matter? Is something wrong?"

"Oh, my back," Yvonne answered as she got to her feet and leaned to stretch her back.

"Oh, my goodness," Mrs. Martin said. "Are you okay? Whatever is wrong? Has something happened to the children? You look so scared."

Yvonne shook her head. "It's the ghost," she explained. "I was frightened by the ghost. I was just about to go up and check the children. You surprised me. I almost jumped out of my skin."

Mr. Martin spoke. "Ghost, what ghost?"

"Didn't you know that you have a ghost in the house?" Yvonne's voice was frantic.

"No, we don't have a ghost," Mr. Martin said. "There's nothing like that here."

"But, the back door keeps opening and closing by itself," Yvonne answered. "I even locked it and it kept doing it. It was a ghost. It was trying to scare me."

"No, dear," Mrs. Martin said, "there's no ghost."

"But, I'm sure it was following me through the house," Yvonne added.

Mrs. Martin seemed to suddenly understand what Yvonne was talking about.

"Oh, that old back door," she said. "No, there's no ghost. We should have told you about that, but we didn't think of it. The catch on the door is broken and the bolt doesn't work."

"We couldn't get it fixed," Mr. Martin said. "The door is crooked on its hinges. We had to order a new door. It'll be installed tomorrow."

"Oh," Yvonne said. It was starting to make sense. There was no ghost. She felt herself calming down. There's nothing to be afraid of, she said to herself.

"We're so sorry," Mrs. Martin said in a comforting tone. "We should have told you about it. We should have at least had it on the list of things to tell you."

Yvonne put her hand on her chest and took a really deep breath. She was starting to feel a whole lot better.

"We have that fancy rock there by the door to keep it closed," Mrs. Martin explained. "Robert, here," she added, as she pointed to her husband, "must have forgotten to place the rock against the door after he took out the trash earlier."

"Oh, my goodness," Yvonne said, as she sat down on the steps. "I was scared half to death. I've never run into a ghost before and I was so afraid I was about to see one."

"I've never seen a ghost either," Mrs. Martin said. "And I hope I never shall."

"Me either," Yvonne agreed and she smiled.

She felt a little silly that she hadn't noticed the rock by the back door. She thought that she should have seen it and wondered what it was for, because, if there was a rock sitting there, she would have tried to figure out the purpose for it. She may have been able to figure it out if she had noticed, but she didn't. She had let her imagination get the better of her.

The End

It was a dark and stormy night ...

Zeke

Zeke was trying to get used to the idea of sharing a room with his brother, Zane. Their parents said it was just a temporary situation. The two brothers were making adjustments, but they looked forward to having their own rooms again. They had never shared a room before.

Zeke had found it necessary to explain his and his brother's unusual names to people many times over the years. He told the story that his parents had told to the brothers. They had heard them tell that story a couple of hundred times – whenever they met someone new who hadn't heard it yet.

Their parents said they met at a pizza parlor. They were both working their way through college by holding jobs at the pizza shop. They said they practically lived on pizza during that time. So, they joked that pizza had helped them survive college and get their degrees. When they got married, they had a giant pizza party for their reception.

Zeke's father called them the 'Pizza' family. He said that when they had twin boys, they suddenly had a very clever idea. They chose the boys' names on purpose because, his name was Paul and their mother was

Irene ... the boys were Zane and Zeke ... and their last name was Andrews. Their father would laugh and say that the initials of their names spelled out PIZZA ... so they became the Pizza family. He said it was *meant to be* ... it was destiny.

The twins weren't so sure they could see the destiny in the idea, especially when they had to explain their names all the time. But, they were so used to their names by now that they couldn't think of any other names they would call themselves if they wanted to change to something else.

Paul had a brother, Uncle Seth, and they weren't twins or anything, but they had always been close. They were both in the military and they were instructors at a big military base in Georgia. When Zeke's father was transferred to a base in Colorado Springs, Colorado, Uncle Seth put in his paperwork to request a transfer also. Uncle Seth was approved but he was still waiting for the paperwork to be finished processing.

In the meantime, the Pizza family moved to the new base in Colorado Springs. They brought Uncle Seth's son, Gene, along with them so he could start at the new school with the twins, since his family would be moving there soon. Uncle Seth wasn't exactly sure how long it would actually be, but he thought it would be soon. He didn't want Gene to be behind everyone else in his work at the new school, so he packed him up and sent him right along with the Pizza family to the new house.

Gene was an only child. Uncle Seth said he didn't want him to be a spoiled brat because he didn't have any brothers or sisters, so Gene had spent a lot of time with Zane and Zeke while they were growing up. They had been asked a million times if they were brothers. The twins were fourteen years old and Gene was thirteen, so they probably did look like brothers.

That was the reason Zeke was *temporarily* sharing a room with his brother. Gene was staying in the room that Zane would have had if Gene wasn't there. Zane would move to his own room after Uncle Seth and Aunt Jeannie got there and moved into their own house. Gene would go home and the room would be available for Zane.

Zeke was listening to the storm outside. It had been raining all day. He was surprised to find out that, when it rained in Colorado, it could be a real 'gully washer' as his father called it. It would suddenly start raining very heavily and the streets would be flooded until the rain stopped and then all the water gushing down the streets would quickly disappear, as if by magic. The thunder and lightning were much more severe than they had ever seen living in Georgia.

Zeke had been standing at the window during a storm the week they arrived. He was looking at the lightning as it streaked all over the sky and, all of a sudden, a huge clap of thunder crashed outside and the force of the noise blew him back from the window. He was stunned at the strength the sound of thunder could have. He decided that he had learned not to stand at the window during a Colorado storm. Zane decided the same thing.

Zeke's father had taken the other two boys to the mall. They wanted to buy new basketball shoes for school.

They joined the team. Zeke had no intention of playing basketball. He would have preferred to play tennis, but the new school didn't have a team.

A guy at school told him the local community center had tennis courts and they had teams that competed against other teams in the city and up in Denver. Zeke intended to look into it.

That was the same guy who said he was friends with the kid who used to live in the house the Pizza family just moved into. He said the kid told him the house was haunted.

Zeke told his mother about it but she said it was just silly nonsense. She said that they had already been there almost two weeks and nothing weird or unusual had happened, so not to worry about it.

Zeke had declined the offer to go with the others to the mall, even when his father hinted that they might go to the movies while they were there. His father knew he really liked movies, and he probably thought that would make him want to go, but Zeke said he didn't want to go out in the storm. Besides, he was building a model car and he wanted to finish it so the glue could dry overnight.

Zeke was listening to the storm outside and reading the instructions for the model car when he thought he heard the sound of tapping. He stopped to listen. Then he heard it again.

It sounded like someone softly tapping on the wall. It made him feel uneasy because there should not have been anyone there to be tapping on the wall. He knew that his mother was still at home, but she was working down in her sewing room, which was downstairs at the far end of the house. If she was tapping, he didn't think that he would hear it all the way upstairs.

Wait! He heard it again! Tap ... tap ... tap! It was spooky. The storm outside was making everything kind of spooky. He put down the paper he had been reading and focused his hearing for any sound. When he hadn't heard it for a few minutes, he decided that he might have imagined it.

Just as he turned his attention back to the model car, he heard the sound again. Tap ... tap ... tap! After just a couple of minutes it sounded once again. Tap ... tap ... tap! What can that be, he wondered? Could it be mice in the walls? Well, it *was* an older house, he said to himself. Didn't older houses usually have mice?

Tap ... tap ... tap! He started to feel creepy. He searched his mind for an answer, for something that sounded like it, so he wouldn't be afraid.

Tap ... tap ... tap! He knew he was definitely *not* imagining that! Then he had a thought ... a ghost! It was a ghost! It was a ghost, tapping on the wall to get his attention. It knew he was alone in the upper part of the house. He was instantly scared at the idea.

What should I do, he asked himself? Should I go downstairs? Should I go sit in the sewing room until the others come home? Do I go tell Mom about it? He knew that wasn't a good idea. She had already said it was nonsense. She wasn't going to believe that a ghost was upstairs tapping on the wall in his bedroom. But, what if it was true? How could he convince her? Would she come upstairs with him and sit in here and wait for the sound?

He didn't really think so. She would say that it must be something else – like a tree branch hitting the house in the wind, or a loose shingle on the roof flapping in the wind. If that were true, then why would it be sounding in threes --- it was always three taps. That didn't make sense.

Tap … tap … tap! There it was again! Zeke slowly got up out of his chair, so as not to make a sound. He didn't want the ghost to know that he was up and moving around in his room.

He crept over to the window on the side of the house. He could see that there were no tree branches touching the house.

Tap … tap … tap! He was scared! He quietly tip toed over to the window which faced the front of the house. He looked out into the front yard. No tree branches were touching the house there either.

He decided that he should go downstairs. He thought that he would feel safer down there – not that he was looking for his mother to protect him or anything – after all, he was old enough to take care of himself. He didn't need his mother to protect him! Still, he thought that he'd feel a lot better if he were down there near her – kind of looking out for her.

He didn't have his shoes on … he was only wearing his socks, so he believed he could sneak out of the room and go down the stairs without the ghost hearing him. He had to chance it.

Tap ... tap ... tap! He was almost too afraid to move. What if he ran into the ghost out in the hall? That kid said the house was haunted. Now, Zeke knew he was right. That wasn't silly nonsense knocking on the wall. It was a ghost! Maybe he *should* tell his mother so they could move out!

Tap ... tap ... tap! Zeke moved silently toward the bedroom door. He could see the stairway, halfway down the hall. It would only take maybe ten steps to be at the top of the stairs, he determined.

His heart was pounding in his chest! He softly stepped through the doorway into the hall. He had only taken a few steps when he was outside Gene's bedroom door. The door was open just a crack.

Tap ... tap ... tap! The sound was coming from inside Gene's room! The ghost must be in there! He wanted to take off running, but he didn't. He stood there for a minute, thinking about what was happening. He couldn't explain it to himself, but his curiosity got the better of him and he decided that he just *had* to have a look. After all, it occurred to him, could a ghost hurt you? It wasn't a physical thing so how could it grab you? Besides, after he saw it, he could always run – he would already be ahead of it. He could race down the stairs before it could catch up with him, he concluded.

Tap ... tap ... tap! There it was again! He was absolutely sure that it was coming from Gene's room. The wall in Gene's room was the same wall in his room, so that made sense to him.

He reached out his hand toward the door. It was ajar, so he thought that he could just push it open, take a quick look, and then run for the stairs. His heart felt like it was in his throat. It was pounding so hard that it was choking him. He could hardly breathe. He tried to calm himself down.

He almost changed his mind. Was this a dumb plan? Was it a really foolish thing to do? Confront a ghost? Yeah, it was stupid, he told himself, but he was already here, so why not. He *had* to be sure so that he could tell his parents why the Pizza family *had* to find another place to live – and they would have to find another place right away ... like immediately ... like today! They weren't going to be able to share this house with a ghost! There might even be a bunch of them! Who knows, he thought, they might have been here for a hundred years!

Tap ... tap ... tap! He took a deep breath and held it. His hand was almost touching the door. He pushed his hand forward until his fingertips were just touching the door.

He felt like he was trembling. Is this what people are talking about when they say 'trembling with fear' in books, he wondered?

He braced himself to be ready to run. With his fingertips, he pressed against the door and slowly pushed it open so that he could see the whole room.

He caught his breath and stepped back! Then a feeling of foolishness washed over him and he let out his breath that it seemed like he had been holding forever. He felt stupid. The Pizza family wouldn't have to move after all.

On the dresser against the wall in Gene's room was Billy, Gene's pet parrot. The cage was set too close to the wall and Billy was pecking at the wall! Zeke thought that he might be agitated because of the storm. He knew that Gene had taught the bird how to tap three times to get a treat.

Duh! Why hadn't he thought of that? It was just Billy. Maybe, he decided, it was because he wasn't used to Billy living in the house. But, he argued with himself, he still should have figured it out.

He made a vow that he would never mention this to Zane – he would *never* hear the end of it.

Zeke went back to his room.

The End

Made in the USA
Las Vegas, NV
04 September 2022